CW00690251

Sublime short stories from Vanessa Gebbie, a master of the art. Meta-fiction, fable, satire, instruction manual, or reportage? Sometimes all in the one story. *A Short History of Synchronised Breathing* is funny, sexy, original, heartbreaking, and with true insights to the human condition.

Vanessa Gebbie is the author of several books, including a novel, short fictions and poetry. Her work has been supported by an Arts Council England Grant for the Arts, a Hawthornden Fellowship and residencies at both Gladstone's Library and Anam Cara Writers' and Artists' Retreat. She teaches widely.

www.vanessagebbie.com

Vanessa Gebbie is also the author of *Memorandum: Poems for the Fallen,* published by Cultured Llama in 2016.

Charming and challenging, inventive and intelligent – a wonderful collection that is also laugh out loud funny.

Paul McVeigh, author of *The Good Son*

A prodigiously gifted writer.

Maggie Gee, author of *Virginia Woolf in Manhattan*

About *The Coward's Tale*:

Gebbie is as at ease with humour as she is with poignancy. A hypnotic debut.

Leila Sanai, *The Independent*

About *Storm Warning*:

...enough good pieces in enough styles for the book to be used as an anthology demonstrating how stories should be written nowadays.

Tim Love's Literary References

For Millie and Arthur

A SHORT HISTORY OF SYNCHRONISED BREATHING
and other stories

A SHORT HISTORY OF SYNCHRONISED BREATHING
and other stories

Vanessa Gebbie (signature)

Vanessa Gebbie

Cultured Llama Publishing

First published in 2017 by
Cultured Llama Publishing
INTRA, 337 - 341 High Street
Rochester, Kent ME1 1DA
www.culturedllama.co.uk

Cultured Llama

ISBN 978-0-9568921-2-6

Printed in Great Britain by Lightning Source UK Ltd

Cover design by Mark Holihan
Cover image painted by Michaela Ridgway
Edited by Anne-Marie Jordan and Maria C. McCarthy

Contents

How Claude Romarin Lost the Buttocks of Celestine Bigorneaux   1

The Properties of Wax   6

Wei-ch'i   12

Letters from the Correspondence of Katerina Liskova, Prague, 1933 onwards   15

Gifts   19

Third Person Singular   22

Pavel's Grey Painting   27

Were It Possible To Just Have Sustenance   30

Ed's Theory of the Soul   34

Taxi   40

Housekeeping   47

Parallax   54

Captain Quantum's Universal Entertainment   59

Selected Advice for Strangers   73

Literary Analysis   78

Snakes and Ladders – Creative Writhing   81

Revisiting Luther   84

Naming Finbar   91

Chapter XXXVIII – Conclusion (and a little bit of added cookery)   95

A Short History of Synchronised Breathing   102

Skellig   116

Acknowledgements   119

How Claude Romarin Lost the Buttocks of Celestine Bigorneaux

There is, in Rue Carnot, a greengrocer's that still bears the name of Claude Romarin. But this is not necessarily a story about greengrocers. This is the story of how the electrification of a small railway led to a most miraculous near-disaster. And it is a story about facts. How, in the wrong hands, they mean nothing.

To the matters of import
It is 1954. The little rack and pinion railway between Chamonix and the great glacier is newly electrified. Our greengrocer, Claude Romarin, now approaching old age, is waiting on the platform. There is also a young man by the name of Dortmund Fallipoux, a student of electrical matters, waiting for the train. He is whistling.

To the matter of the greengrocer
Claude Romarin is a tender lover to his wife of many years, the sturdy and bewhiskered Helga Romarin, whose

hands are now permanently blackened thanks to years of immersion in sacks of potatoes. However, he has a history. When an apprentice greengrocer, Claude Romarin fell in love, not with Helga, or any part of Helga, but with the buttocks of a young flibbertigibbet by the name of Celestine Bigorneaux.

To the matter of Celestine's buttocks
Bending down in an orange skirt in 1919, selecting a demi-kilo of carrots from an open sack, to the young Claude, her buttocks resembled a perfectly rounded pumpkin. The youth, aware of the softness of the flesh of a ripe pumpkin, fled to the privacy of the potato store to overcome his tension. And, since that formative ejaculatory moment, the memory of the buttocks of Celestine Bigorneaux (who moved to Frejus and became a film star, appearing in at least three films, two with a speaking line) has been a vital prelude to any form of relaxation. Including making love to his wife. An occurrence which, thanks to her hirsute nature, has become a challenge. Claude Romarin is in the habit of working his way into the moment via thoughts of firm, ripe, orange pumpkins, via Celestine Bigorneaux's buttocks and memories of the potato store, to…

To the matter of the train. Which has arrived at the station, and also departed, in the space of the last page
There are only two passengers in this compartment. Claude Romarin himself and the student of electrical matters, Dortmund Fallipoux. They are sitting opposite each other on metal benches. The rack and pinion has just taken the weight of the train, and new overhead wires are delivering measured amounts of electricity to the mechanism. This is a single track railway; there is a crossing point half way up, to allow for the downward train to pass the upward. Or vice versa.

To the matter of the crossing point

Here, there is a surge of electricity. A simple matter caused by the proximity of a little brown wire to a yellow, or perhaps the other way round, but it happens just as the greengrocer is beginning a daydream about pumpkins (and by extension, buttocks), and the student is immersing himself in a textbook. There is a hiss and a sparking outside the carriage, and a slight smell of singeing within. And…

Pouf! They are gone! The buttocks!

Instead, this is in Romarin's head:

The line has a gradient varying from 11 to 22% and is equipped with rack rail. The line is electrified using an overhead line at 11,000 volts.

Dortmund Fallipoux suddenly blinks. 'Pumpkins?' he says. 'Where are my facts, my formulae?'

Romarin does not answer, so bemused is he by electrical detail:

The hertz is the SI unit of frequency. Its base unit is s1. One hertz means 'one cycle per second', 100 hertz means 'one hundred cycles per second'. The unit may be applied to any periodic event. A human heart may be said to beat at 1.2 Hz.

The student leans forward. 'Monsieur,' he says, his face contorted with worry. 'I know nothing about pumpkins, and yet…'

'The frequency of aperiodic events, such as radioactive decay, are expressed in becquerels,' announces Claude Romarin.

'Such firm and rounded pumpkins,' sighs the student, smiling. 'So very…' he searches for the right word. 'So very orange.'

'You, Sir,' says Claude Romarin, seeing the student's face, 'have stolen my buttocks.'

'And you, Sir,' retorts the student, 'have stolen my homework.'

Claude Romarin shuts his eyes, but no buttocks can he conjure. Just:

A disc rotating at 1 revolution per minute can be said to be rotating at 0.105 rad/s or 0.017 Hz, where the latter reflects the number of complete revolutions per second.

It is not a long journey to the Mer de Glace. At the top is a café where walkers can seek refreshment, still.

'I propose a small Pastis while we decide what to do about pumpkins and electrical details,' says Claude Romarin.

'I know nothing of electrical details,' mourns the student of electrical details.

'Let me tell you,' says Claude, taking the student by the arm, walking with him towards the café. 'The usual waveform of an AC power circuit is a sine wave, Monsieur, as this results in the most efficient transmission of energy. However, in certain applications, different waveforms are used, such as triangular or square waves...'

Dortmund Fallipoux is reduced to tears.

To matters of concern to Dortmund Fallipoux

Here he is, holding textbooks regarding electricity – about which he knows precisely nothing. He is contemplating a career in market gardening, specialising in pumpkins.

To matters of concern to Claude Romarin

Claude is now conversant with many details, facts and statistics, but understands them not one whit. And what good are facts if they are not to be applied? Moreover, at the back of his mind is his husbandly duty to Helga. How can he approach his wife without first consulting the ... whatever they were ... of Celestine Bigorneaux? It is impossible that Alessandro Volta, who invented the Voltaic Pile ... will ever make an effective aphrodisiac.

Several Pastis later, the train being ready to depart, both gentlemen again board the train, and sit opposite each other on metal benches. The student's head is full of pumpkins (which of course he is completely misusing, lighting them from within by wax candles), and Claude Romarin's head is stuffed with enough relevant facts to start a hydro-electric power plant … if he did but understand them.

To matters at the crossing point

Whether it is the proximity of a little yellow wire to a blue, or vice versa, or whether Le Bon Dieu in his infinite wisdom decides to replace the correct memories in the respective heads of a young student and an old man, is not recorded. But, just as Claude Romarin is pondering the breakdown of electricity providers throughout France, and just as Dortmund Fallipoux is inventing a new recipe for pumpkin soup, there is again a hissing and a sparking outside the carriage, and the faintest – the very faintest – smell of singeing, within.

Dortmund Fallipoux sighs, leans his head against the window, and goes back to his books. And Claude Romarin sighs, closes his eyes, and dreams of running his hands over a pumpkin, which, of course, becomes warm and pliant under his touch.

Tout va bien. On reaching Chamonix, they shake hands a little warily, and part company.

Epilogue

Dortmund Fallipoux graduated with distinction in 1958 and became the youngest ever Directeur of l'EDF (L'Electricité de France). It is said that he never liked pumpkins in any form, raw or cooked.

Claude Romarin lived happily with Helga for another eight years, after which, following a short illness, he died. And it is a safe bet that on his deathbed, he did not spend his last conscious moments on matters electrical.

5

The Properties of Wax

At first, Khun Kamsak wanted nothing to do with Chaung
Lawan's plan. But money speaks in a persuasive voice.
Eventually he said, with a slight cough, although he did
not seem to have a chill, that it would take a week to model, as he put it, 'a particular part of your dead husband, a
most private part, in wax.'

'Why a week?' said Lawan, tucking her credit card
into her sleeve, picking up her basket, ready to resume
her round of the market stalls. Kamsak stared at the small
grey-haired woman who was looking at him over the shop
counter with her head on one side as though she was listening for distant birdsong.

'Because I must arrange access, you understand,' he
said. 'Because it is a certainty that such an unusual request
will be the subject of a delay. Questions will be asked.
And they must be answered. And besides, I must arrange
the correct wax.' And, he explained, he could not use the
standard wax, oh no – he needed something more malleable, more translucent, more … realistic.

Lawan pulled a paper from her sleeve. 'My Aroon's

body is here,' she said, sliding the paper across the counter. Kamsak took it and adjusted his spectacles.

'Khon Kaen is a good distance,' he said. 'Your husband died in Khon Kaen?'

'He did. It was most thoughtless of him.' Lawan sighed. Then, perhaps, thinking better of herself, 'Visiting his brother.'

'I will need travel expenses,' the creator of wax models said, suddenly businesslike.

Lawan smiled. 'Of course. When I collect the item, perhaps?'

Lawan was a prudent woman. It was, of course, not possible for Lawan to explain. But that night, curled on her side, trying with no success to sleep in the bed that was now as empty as a field after drought, her hand crept behind her back, and her fingers closed on air. How would it have been possible for an elderly woman to look Khun Kamsak (waxwork models a speciality) in the eye, and talk about sleeping with her Aroon – her Nu-nu – for many years? But if it had been possible, she would have said, 'I would have you know, Khun Kamsak, that when we were younger, my Nu-nu and I had relations every single night. Occasionally, twice.'

Kamsak would have pushed his spectacles up his nose and laid his palms on the counter. 'Well, naturally, Chaung Lawan, I remember your Aroon well as a younger man. In fact I recall very well him telling me about … his prowess, you understand…'

Lawan would have raised an eyebrow and patted her hair. 'The prowess was shared, I can assure you,' and she would have looked out at the market, and then back at the model-maker. 'Indeed, I had a good teacher, a friend who was a worker at the Eden Club. Very accomplished woman, one of the most in demand…' Lawan would have lowered her eyes here and made the slightest of movements with her hands, her mouth, her hips.

Then she would have sighed. 'But, Kamsak, we are both old, are we not? You not quite as old as I, I think, but not far off?'

Kamsak would have smiled. Waved a hand towards his certificates. 'I have some years of work in me yet,' he would have said. 'Many models still to make.'

Lawan would have remained grave. 'I wish you many years of good work.' And then she would have collected herself, remembered why she was there. 'Our bodies grow old, but our hearts do not, Kamsak. And this model, you will take the utmost care? Every fold of skin, every curve?' Kamsak would have looked nonplussed.

'But of course. It will be a perfect replica of the real item. This is why I need the most special wax. The most delicate, the most malleable, the most realistic.' He paused. 'The most expensive.' Then Lawan would have allowed herself to smile. And she would have opened her fingers on his counter, relaxing them, so they fell into the most natural, welcoming shape.

Lawan called into Kamsak's workshop every other day. Every visit, he looked up and shook his head, except on a single occasion when another man was working behind the counter, and looked at her blankly. But on the eighth day, Kamsak was there, gestured to her and smiled. 'Come in, Chaung Lawan. Your commission is ready.' And he bowed and disappeared into his workshop. Lawan put her basket down by the counter and breathed in the scents of warm wax.

Kamsak returned with a small package. 'Shall I?'

'Of course,' Lawan said. 'I always inspect my purchases.'

He smiled and unwrapped the package. Inside was a Perspex box. And inside the box, lying on a small, green cushion, perfectly formed in the most expensive wax, was a particular part of her late Aroon. A most precious part.

'May I see?' Lawan asked.

'Of course, please…' Kamsak handed her the box and Lawan held it to the light. The most precious part of her late husband peered back at her. The dorsal vein was raised very slightly. It lay in a slight curve, as though it was asleep. She held the box reverentially. She held it close to her face, peering carefully, to see if it really was. It was. And it was perfect.

'Very good, very good,' said Lawan. She put the box down. Suddenly she felt very tired. She would go home, and may not even put the shopping away. She would eat something then go to their bed, hers and Nu-nu's, and she would lie down. She would turn on her side, imagining Nu-nu's warmth curved behind her. She would take the Perspex box, and would open it very, very carefully. She would lift the precious part from its little green cushion and maybe she'd give it his special name, 'Nu-nu,' she'd whisper. 'I have missed you.' Then she would creep her hand behind her back, settle the item in the palm of her hand, as she had done for decades, after certain activities, of course – and when the precious part had been attached to her husband – and she would drift to sleep.

'Chaung Lawan? My travel expenses?'

'Forgive me. I was dreaming.'

'I will wrap it for you,' said Kamsak, taking a sheet of tissue paper.

Lawan placed the little package carefully in her basket. 'I cannot thank you enough.' Lawan was half way out of the door, when she heard a cough. She turned, her basket heavy in her hand, but Kamsak was no longer looking at her. He was only opening a drawer behind his counter.

Back in the apartment, Lawan made herself a quick supper in the kitchenette, and did not tidy away the dishes. They could wait. She prepared herself for the night, and sat on the edge of the bed to open the Perspex box.

Her eyelids felt like wax themselves, warm, coated and heavy. 'Tonight, Nu-nu,' Lawan whispered, 'you and I will sleep well.' But try as she would, with her old fingers, she could not open the box. She could not find where the lid would lift. Her fingers could not feel any irregularity in the Perspex that might indicate a closure. Lawan crossed to the window, and held the box up in the glare of the streetlight. Nothing. Her old eyes could not make out the means of opening the box. Not even in this bright light. The box was completely sealed.

Back in the kitchenette, she placed the box on the table. She put the electric ring back on, selected a knife with a thin blade, and held the blade against the heat until the knife handle began to burn her palm. She tried the knife against the Perspex, and it made an indent, but not enough to pierce the material. She would have to get the knife red hot, would need to hold the handle with a cloth. And would need to take such care that her hand did not tremble when she levered the top of the box away. She would need something –matchsticks perhaps – to keep the edges from resealing themselves.

'Oh, Nu-nu. I am too old for this. Why did you not let me go first?'

There was no answer.

Lawan wrapped the knife handle round in a piece of towelling, and held the blade across the ring. She blew on the ring, and the blade, as she had seen the metal workers do on their stalls. And slowly, the blade began to redden as the heat rose against her cheek.

She pressed the knife edge again and again with the utmost care against the edges of the lid, and coughed as her nose was filled with acrid fumes. Then tiny black wisps rose into the air like souls from open mouths and, hovered over the table as the Perspex melted, gradually giving up the lid.

Lawan lay down on the mattress, and curled onto her side. Aroon's most precious part lay waiting on its little green cushion. She could feel herself falling asleep already as she reached into the box with trembling fingers.

Thinking back later, Lawan could not even recall putting her hand behind her back. Or consciously remembering the intimacy of sleeping curled into each other as they grew old, Aroon's precious part held gently in her fingers, as she had for years. She must have fallen immediately into the deepest of sleeps, from which she awoke next morning to find she hadn't even moved. She lay on her side, one hand below her cheek. The other, behind her, still holding Aroon.

'Good morning, Nu-nu,' Lawan mouthed, stretching a little. Then she moved her arm, to bring his part where she could see it, where she could lay it back on its cushion ready for tonight. She opened her fingers.

But all that remained was a misshapen handful of wax, bearing the imprint of her own closed hand, indents for her fingers, every fold and line of her old skin. Every wrinkle. Even the scar where she'd cut her finger as a girl over seventy years ago. Indeed, the only smooth surface left was the line where Lawan's wedding ring had cut deep into the wax, a simple curve, unwavering and straight.

Wei-Ch'i

Shaozu's apartment seemed further away this evening. As usual, the battered grey bus dropped him with the other workers at the intersection and he walked the rest. But his old feet seemed heavier than yesterday. Even the air in his empty lunch bag weighed down his shoulder.

Huang was crouched in the doorway, throwing knucklebones in the dust. He looked up at Shaozu.

'Sometime, we must come to the end of all possible permutations,' he said.

The air in the apartment was still. Perhaps Mei was out. Perhaps she had gone to the late market, or left a note to say there was a last-minute game of Wei-Ch'i.

But on the table in the kitchenette, Shaozu found no note. Instead, in a room in which everything had been put in its correct place, cloths neatly folded, platters arranged in careful pyramids, he found something else.

Mei's hand.

It instilled no panic. Not even a sense of worry. The hand lay quite peacefully palm up, the fingers curled like a half open lotus. There was no blood; not a single drop. It might have been a waxwork. But it was definitely Mei's hand. There was her plain gold band, the small scar on the index finger. And there on every single nail was the clear varnish from their anniversary dinner, chipped, where only this morning she'd been scraping at a thumbnail with the index nail of the other hand.

Shaozu walked round the table peering at the hand. It mattered that he should know which hand this was. The one whose thumbnail had been scraped, or the one whose index had done the scraping.

And it mattered that the hand was alone.

Shaozu thought of calling to his wife. He thought of standing in the kitchenette and calling, 'Mei? I have found your hand…,' but there was something quite wrong with that, as though he would be disturbing a shrine.

In the hallway, he found her right foot. He had walked straight past it, lined up neatly beside her sandals. He crouched and put out a tentative hand. The foot was cool. Picking it up, he returned to the kitchenette and placed the foot on the table next to the hand. After all, the wrong partner was better than no partner at all. Loneliness is a dreadful thing.

Slowly, Shaozu moved through the apartment, searching. He found Mei everywhere. Her legs below the knee, one in the shower room, one on the balcony. Her arms, one in the drawer of the console table, one on a kitchen shelf. A shoulder, high in the hallway on top of the cupboard where they kept their outdoor clothes.

He found her stomach, rounded as a child's, on the pillow in the spare bedroom. The room where, very occasionally, their son slept when his work brought him to the city.

Shaozu picked up each part with care, bringing them all into the kitchenette, laying them together on the table. He did not try to reassemble her. He laid them in the general order in which he found the parts, as that seemed proper.

For a while Shaozu was unable to go to the room where he and Mei had slept for forty years. He found his eyes pricking. He found himself recalling Mei's voice the other night, over dinner:

'My husband. I have something to tell you.'

And her quiet life-litany. A marriage agreed to for money. A lack.

In the bedroom, he hoped he might find two things. Mei's little face with its bright eyes and high cheekbones. And her heart. But some things, no matter how close they may have been, are never found at all.

Letters from the Correspondence of Katerina Liskova, Prague, 1933 onwards

Dear Secretary to the Controller of Pedestrian Ways,

I am returning your flower.

As you see, one petal must have become detached in transit, and that I have kept, purely for the colour. It looks well on a small, white linen handkerchief – one I keep in its box exactly as it was sent to me, a long time ago now.

I have to say, I was not ready for the dreams that accompanied the flower. You must be the most disturbed person if you do not mind me making that observation. For the last three nights, while the flower was next to my bed, I dreamed of road-mending. And brick walls. And roof timbers carved with small animals on the sides – carvings that could never ever be seen except by a very small child crawling against his parents' wishes, and in not inconsiderable danger, up in the rafters.

With best wishes,

K

Dear Secretary to the Controller of Pedestrian Ways,

One July, a long time ago, I sat at the dining table with my husband's hand on my stomach, willing movement to happen. Slowly, when no signs appeared, and other signs reappeared, I knew I had never carried a child. I had simply been ill.

Many years later, I was ill again. There was no thought of children – it was far too late. I was taken to a small hospital. I cannot remember much, forgive me – I spent my days in a haze – but I do remember the bed on which I lay was metal, and the paint on the bed-head was cracked, leaving an unpainted patch, a shape that resembled Italy. At first, I did not understand the presence of this shape, but one day, I awoke with a pain such as I had never experienced before. I am not given to screaming, but I believe I did so – and was told to hold on to the bed-head for relief. My fingers felt for the shape of Italy. I thus shared my pain with all those who had been there before me.

I truly believed I was dying. I dreamed in bouts of fitful sleep, and saw a great axe bearing down. The doctors drawing a line in black paint down my stomach where the pain was worst – exactly where the axe was to fall.

I gave birth to our son. Perfect in every way, Secretary. The child conceived all those years before, and forgotten by his mother. Denied. And I will always wonder if it was this that caused that half-death – but I finally gave birth to the child who had waited all that time. And who, in the waiting, had been protected by a coat of stone. A stone baby.

Have you heard of stone babies, Secretary? It is rare, I believe. But I daresay there are medical books that deal with the subject. Suffice it to say – my son had waited thirty years to be born, and first saw the light of day through stone eyes.

I called him Gregor, after his father. He was perfect, as far as one can ascertain. I did not let the doctors perform an autopsy. There was no need. There was a man there, who had visited remote regions of the Caucasus mountains, and had seen such things for himself. Gregor was simply a five-month child, curled into himself as though he were sleeping, one hand stretched over his head, holding his ear.

I find it hard to write this.

Stone had covered him completely. For some reason, the layers were thickest and ridged over his body so that he resembled a large carapace. His colour was dark. Over time, he had blackened, and the texture of his covering was a little shiny. Like the surface of a bone long buried in rich soil.

My son was beautiful.

With best wishes,

K

Dear Secretary to the Controller of Pedestrian Ways,

Margarethe and the farmer went away for two nights. His mother was unwell and they went to find out how close to the end she might be. There has been talk of inheritance over breakfast for a week.

When they had gone, I became like a child. The house was for me and me alone. I went upstairs to my old bedroom, and opened the window. I took the bedding off the bed, and bundled everything together in a cupboard, then I let the room air for half a day. I swept the boards, and removed everything of theirs from the drawers, putting them elsewhere. And I remade the bed with my bedding from the kitchen alcove.

I spent time in my old vegetable garden, weeding and straightening, and after supper, I took my child, Gregor, and I put him on a shelf where he could see out over the garden, over the fields to the hills. The mantel where he normally sits has no view – only of a room, dark with smoke much of the time. Only lit when the door is opened.

In bed that night, I began to think of letters, and why we write them at all. I began to think about whether anyone will ever write the definitive letter, after which there will be no need to write anything. Ever.

I wondered if one day there would be an invention (I ought to have studied to be an engineer – I would have invented wonderful things) – a letter that would have all possible permutations of sounds impregnated into the paper. And the sender would only have to let the paper know of their emotional state, and events to be communicated, questions to be asked, and so forth, and the letter would form itself in transit.

Of course, problems might come when the letter had news of great sadness to impart because then, it would not be easy to form the necessary sounds. I am sure that paper has the same vestigial understanding of emotion as did the trees from which it was made. Think back, Secretary, to the field belonging to my good friend. And the crop in the field that would not grow unless it was watched. The crop, each small ear of corn, of wheat, each potato plant knew what it was to be valued. And if they can do so, how much more can a tree?

And then it came to me. In all the many letters we have sent to each other, in all those thousands upon thousands of words, there is every possible permutation, is there not? Were all our words to be rearranged, they might spell out totally different messages – and yet they would still be words written from me to you, or vice versa. That begs the question – what is truth?

With best wishes,

K

Gifts

Diary entry: Saturday, November 18th

Got a package. Twenty inches by twelve, wrapped in brown paper, slightly misshapen, narrower at one end than the other. Not particularly heavy. No addressee. Nothing. I wasn't expecting anything. I was just going to do some gardening. I shouted back into the house, 'Edna? Expecting a package?'

She shouted back no she wasn't, then appeared, wiping her hands on a cloth. 'Is it for us?'

'It doesn't say.'

Edna shook her head. We weren't the sort of people to get packages, she said. It was probably for the neighbours. Not the Franklins, they were away. She said she was busy.

I picked up the package. It wasn't heavy – but solid. I took it across to the Murdoch's, and rang the bell. There was no answer, even though the car was in the drive, and the upstairs curtains were closed.

So I left the package on their doorstep, and went back to the gardening. After a while, Murdoch came out and stood looking at it. Then he saw me. 'Did you leave this here?'

I nodded.

'It's not for us,' I said.

'What is it?'

'No idea. We aren't expecting anything.'

Murdoch went back inside, leaving the package on the doorstep. That made me cross. He should have at least opened it, seen what it was. I stuck the spade in the soil, went and knocked. He came to the door. I nodded at the package. 'Aren't you going to open it?'

'Nope. Nothing to do with me.' He went back inside and shut the door.

I needed to get on with the garden. It wasn't the right time of year to leave it; things get on top of you if you don't deal with them quickly.

I left the package outside the Elias's and went back to my gardening. She did needlework. Maybe the package was for her quilting, something like that.

After a while, Clara Elias came over, carrying the package in both hands like it was alive. 'George left yesterday,' she said. George was a salesman. Photographic.

I nodded. 'Where to?'

'No – he's left. Gone. Taken his stuff. I don't want this.' She put the package down on the grass.

'Don't leave it there. It's not mine.'

'But I saw you bring it a while back.'

'It must be for someone round here.'

Edna called from inside, 'Leonard, who's that?'

Clara Elias had gone. 'No-one', I said.

My hands were muddy now. I took off my boots, went back into the house. Couldn't pick up the package with muddy hands. When I came back out, there was a hearse outside number eleven. The back of the hearse was open, there were flowers. The door to number eleven was closed. It stayed like that for about ten minutes, no-one came out of the house, and no-one seemed to be looking after the hearse.

I took the package across the road and put it in the

back of the hearse, behind a wreath that said 'Gloria' in white chrysanthemums. I don't know who Gloria was. The Roberts at number eleven are called Harry and Margaret. Before I got the bulbs in, the hearse drove off with the package. Just one man driving – I don't know who he was.

I saw a beetle on the lawn. Nothing else of note.

Third Person Singular

This guy crashed into my head this morning, early. My day off, too, sod's law. Must have got in through an eardrum. I said go away there's only room for one middle-aged bloke in here – my brain's shrinking – but he said, no chance, mate.

Seems like he's here to stay. So I ignored him at first. Made a coffee, went to the study. I have a paper to write. That's not work, it's something light for a journal in the US. I do a lot of those these days. Kath doesn't mind. She goes to the theatre, the gym, out for dinner with her mates, talks women's stuff, I guess – when she's not working.

Then this bloke started talking. 'I don't like coffee in the morning, Mike,' he said. Scots accent. 'How's about a nice cup of...'

'Shut it,' I said. 'If you're living in my brain, you do what I do, OK?'

'OK,' he said, 'but I take two sugars – '

'Bog off,' I said.

Anyway. I switch on the world, sit down. With my coffee.

I start to write my paper. In First Person. 'I believe that in the twenty-first century, metallurgy has a vital role to play. I think we are at one of the most exciting times for the industry. I have been –'

'What's that for?' this bloke said.

'Will you just curl up somewhere and die?' I said.

'Nope. What's all this "I, I, I, me, me, me" stuff?'

Oh, right. Fine. A parasite who doesn't know his Persons.

'First Person reporting,' I said. 'It has great immediacy, intimacy on paper. Now leave me to it.'

'First Person?' he said, like he was asking the biggest question the world. 'Intimacy on paper?' he said, in italics. (Now there's a thought. What IS the biggest question in the world?)

I sighed. And gave him a lengthy explanation that would grace the best English and how-she-is-spoke-and-wrote manual.

There was this pause. Deep.

'But...,' he said.

'Oh fer fuck's sake,' I said. 'First person. I. Me. Moi. I mean me. I'm being someone, using a device. Now let me be someone.'

'OK, I'll just watch,' he said

Is there anything worse? Being watched, I mean. Do you think Michelangelo could have painted God's fingers on that ceiling if someone was lying with him up on the scaffolding and saying, 'Ha ha – missed a bit, Buonarotti'?

Did this bloke just watch? Did he hell. Kept asking questions.

'First Person,' he said. 'Like Schumacher? Tiger Woods? Rooney? Best Man? Prime Minister? So whose First Person are you exactly?'

Well that had me thinking. Of course, I'm Kath's First Person. Kath says she loves me now and again at bedtime – we have been married a long while, can't expect miracles. She does say it every morning at 8.05 though.

''Bye, Mike,' she says, dipping, peeking in the hall mirror, patting her hair, picking up the briefcase. 'Love you.' Clever the way she says it over her shoulder like that. (I put up the hall mirror. I'm shorter than Kath.) Sometimes I watch her looking in the rear view mirror, flicking her hair back down, shaking her head.

The dog loves me. I'm the dog's First Person. Blitzen. Shitzen Blitzen, the Shi Tzu. Getting old now, losing control of his sphincter, bit like me … but know something, I love him to bits. Couldn't think of anyone else who'd consider Mike Golightly as their First Person, and that's a bit scary. So I switched the paper into Second Person.

'Metallurgy in the twenty-first century,' I wrote. 'If you consider …'

'What's that?' says this voice. 'Are you talking to me?'

'No,' I said. 'Go to sleep. Second Person. You. Thee, if we were yonks ago. But we're not, and this work needs doing.'

There was silence for a nanosecond.

'If you're talking to me,' he said, 'and it's Second Person … then … I'm the Second Person, aren't I? And you're First. This is neat. I think we're getting somewhere.'

'You may be,' I said. 'Me, I've got a helluva lot to get through.'

'Must be time for another coffee,' he said.

So I made another coffee. Well. Once the idea of coffee's in there, you have to scratch the itch. He chatted away to me in the kitchen like we were old buddies. Said we'd met. Three years back, at one of Kath's office 'dos'. Brian Macnab, he said, and put the idea of Orange Club biscuits into my head.

Brian Macnab. Oh sure. Him. Had Kath blushing like a teenager. Habit of leaning into her, too close. I said something and she told me to back off, he was like that with all the girls.

Half way through the Club biscuit, he said, '…almost as good as sugar.'

'What?' I said.

'I like Orange Clubs.'

'Can you taste it?' I said.

'Sure can,' he said. Then he changed the subject. 'So – I'm Second Person, and you're First Person. That right?'

He hadn't got the faintest idea. Besides which, I needed a piss. All that coffee. I got up, went to the lav. And stood there. Could hear 'Ha Ha, Buonarotti' somewhere … this twat commenting on the books and pictures in the lav.

'Are you watching me?' I said.

'Not exactly,' he said. 'Although it's difficult not to, you know?'

That got me. That's all I needed. 'How the fuck am I meant to piss with some wanker in my ear watching?' I said.

'True,' he said. 'And the other thing.'

'Huh?'

'Nemmind. I'll turn my back.' His voice dimmed a bit. 'Nice hallway,' he said (I'd left the door open). 'Not sure about the statue.'

My pride and joy, that statue. Sculpting for the Spatially Challenged, one term only, half price, local Tertiary. Kath hated it. Said it looked like seventeen of Blitzen's turds (before they went runny) soldered together.

'Can you solder shit?' I said. She didn't answer. Used my statue as something to chuck her anorak over at weekends.

'That statue is unique,' I said.

'Sure is,' said Macnab. I could picture him now. Thinning on top, wearing a dark jacket, silly tie, Daffy Duck cufflinks. No woman could possibly take that seriously.

We went back to the study. I kept quiet. So did he. I started typing. 'The twenty-first century metallurgist lives in exciting times. He or she works in many theatres, many scenarios, has many objectives –'

'What's that?' Macnab said.

'Third Person,' I said. 'He. She. It. A metallurgist.'

'That's interesting. Third Person. Never heard of that.'

'Oh sure,' I said. 'It's the most popular. The most ordinary. Everyone does Third Person.'

'Do they? So who's the Third Person?'

'Anyone,' I said. 'Not me or you, but he or she. See?'

'Think so,' he said. 'Or could you say, not me or she, but you?'

'Nope,' I said, and could have gone on. I could have given him a lecture on the use of persons, cause and effect of persons, limitation of persons, but there was no time.

There was no time because Kath came home. Stood in the hallway red-eyed, stunned, a deer caught in headlights. 'Oh, I forgot you were home today,' she said, and dropped her jacket over the statue. I left it there.

I went to her. Put my hand up, but couldn't touch her. It didn't feel right. 'What's up?' I said.

She went upstairs, didn't speak. I went to follow her. 'Want a coffee? A tea? Glass of something?'

'Later, maybe,' she said, over her shoulder, like the mornings. 'Someone I cared about at work just died. Give me a minute, OK?'

In the study, it was quiet. Until this Scots voice said, 'Run that past me again, Mike. That Third Person thing?'

Pavel's Grey Painting

Pavel's uncle has left him a painting in his will. Pavel is delighted; his uncle was a connoisseur. Pavel waits to see which one has been picked for him.

It is wrapped in plain brown paper. The courier makes Pavel sign, 'Signature, please,' before handing it over. There is layer upon layer of brown paper. Pavel has already taken down his framed accountancy qualification certificates to make space for his new acquisition.

Voilà. But oh, what a choice. His uncle had paintings of magnificent tigers and elephants, castles and mountains – and here is a pale portrait in several shades of grey. An emaciated Jew (Pavel can tell this much) lying on a pile of corpses, eating a shoe.

'Oh, Uncle, what a disappointment.'

Pavel replaces his certificates on the wall. What is entertaining about this painting? What is there in it to up-lift Pavel at the end of a day at the Town Council offices where he is Assistant Deputy Chief Financial Controller?

Rewrapping the painting, Pavel sees a small label on the back. 'The artist. Of course. And his address. It is a good canvas. He can repaint it.'

The artist receives Pavel on a Saturday, Shabbat, making allowances for Pavel's position. He is a small, fine-featured man, and, were Pavel a writer, he might say the artist has the skeleton of a bird. As it is, he thinks the man is small and dark, living in a series of small dark rooms.

Pavel unwraps the painting. The artist takes it, holds it to what light there is. 'This,' he says. 'Selling this was like selling my own liver.'

'Good heavens,' says Pavel. 'Your liver? That would mean death, surely?'

'Yes,' says the artist, who cries openly. 'This was the first painting I sold. I used to destroy everything, sold nothing. But this…'

'Why did you not destroy this one?' says Pavel.

'This one?' says the artist, making a small movement with his hand as though to stroke the work, but pulling back. 'This is my father.'

'Good heavens,' says Pavel. He checks his watch. It is 11:58 a.m., and the supermarket shuts at 13.00 hours. If he is to go to the supermarket, do a whole week's shop before it shuts, he needs to get a move on. 'I would like you to paint over it.'

The artist does not speak. He holds the canvas as though it were a child.

'I will replace it with another canvas,' he says.

But that is not convenient for Pavel. He wishes to keep the canvas bequeathed to him by his uncle, and says so. 'Can you do this in, say, a week? I rather thought I would like an elephant.'

There is a pause. 'An elephant?' says the artist. 'You would have me overpaint my father so?'

'Indeed,' says Pavel. 'Or if not you, perhaps you can suggest some other painter who is able to paint elephants?'

There is another pause. 'If anyone is to do this,' says the artist. 'It must be me.'

Pavel leaves, having made an appointment to collect his new painting on the following Saturday.

For three days and three nights, the artist lives once more with his father. Then he sets the work on an easel and mixes, very carefully, oil paints in several shades of grey, the same shades, in fact, that he used once before.

Were It Possible To Just Have Sustenance

At the end of that little alley, just there, out of the sun, away from the bustle and bluster of the square, is a café. No sign. You have to know it's there. There is no menu. You eat what the kitchen provides.

You push open the door, walk in with a few dead leaves. A small man in a white shirt shows you to a table facing the door, asks if he can take your coat. You say no. It's verging on cold; you might keep it round your shoulders. There's no-one else here. Tables waiting like empty stages, chairs neat. Glasses glinting in the half-light.

Your table is not perfect; a small brown stain on the cloth. You wonder if you should move. After all, you are not alone now, there's the space left in the air by the maker of that brown stain.

The discomfort is slight. No matter. You order a demi-carafe of red.

Just then, the daylight flickers as when a memory marches over your thoughts.

The door is flung open. A man, late middle age, greying, sweating, thin, long raincoat, clutching a trilby to his chest in one hand, in the other a bunch of roses wrapped in brown paper. His shoes are dusty. The door slams shut behind him, and he leans against it, breathing fast, his breath making the briefest of clouds. He glances over his shoulder.

The waiter approaches. 'Monsieur?'

The new arrival reaches out, grasps the waiter by the shirt sleeve.

'Still they line them up, Maurice. Still they ask for volunteers to take rifles and shoot them, those in the lines.'

'Monsieur, it is quiet here. If Monsieur will permit…?' and he takes the shaking man by the elbow, leads him to a corner table, where the poor man sits, his back to you, still holding his hat and his roses. He looks up at the waiter, wipes his eyes on his sleeve like a child.

'I must be in the line at two thirty-five, Maurice.'

You look at the door. Surely the man is mad. Talking of such things and on a day like today, when the sun is shining and the church bells ring out over Paris, sending flocks of birds skyward with each peal?

You want to say to the waiter, look, this is meant to be a good café. I am here on recommendation. But the door opens again.

There is a blast of warmth, as though the sun has thrown a blazing hoop round the earth and it ends rolling on the cobbles of this alley, just here. A woman enters, followed by two more. Dressed in feathered costumes, head dresses askew. Heels clicking on the tiled floor, their laughter making a thick layer in the air. And two more. Five women in feathers, bringing with them a smell of resin, perfume, sweat – their colours brilliant and wicked. Their painted nails flashing, long and sharp.

'Garçon?' someone calls.

The waiter appears with a carafe of red for the thin man.

'Ah, Maurice,' calls one of the women … the one who has pushed to the front, whose laugh is a little louder then the others. The brood fall back to allow her space.

'Madame. Ça va?'

'Maurice. Such a fine procession … but exhausting! Did you hear the bands? The crowds were so thick we could not get through to you. We are so late. Did you keep our table?' Her nails seem to drip, ooze. You blink.

The waiter makes a show of directing the women to a large table. It has a plastic sign, 'Reserved'.

They descend on the table in their feathers, squawking, and make an ostentatious play of taking off their head-dresses, placing them carefully on the table next to yours. You raise your head, but they do not acknowledge you. You do not want to sit surrounded by plumage. It moves. The fronds move like seaweed. It disturbs.

'Du vin,' someone says, and the air relaxes. The feathers are still, but they must be watched.

The thin man watches the window, shaking. Holding his roses and his hat in one hand, now. He takes frantic sips of wine as though it might be the source of his salvation.

You smooth the white cloth. You look round for the waiter. After all, you were first here, you do not yet have a drink, you would appreciate an excuse to move a glass over the brown stain.

There is such a noise; a twittering from the women, a plangent moaning from the thin man. You feel righteous not to be adding to the noise, and therefore you cannot call for Maurice.

Even this disturbs. Why could he not stay 'a waiter'? Now he has a name. Without you wishing it, he has become part of your theatre. Part of your cast, not merely your audience, which was his place.

The door opens again. Two men with two dogs, slim-hipped dogs with muzzles. One man, barrel-chested and short, the other dressed as a judge, long wig, buckled shoes.

'Who won?' they ask. No-one answers.

Beyond the limp half-curtains, the brickwork on the wall is a mass of creeping shadows. The women look up. The thin man moans.

You wait for the waiter.

The two men find themselves a table and the dogs sink to the floor, shivering. One dog has a crusted eye.

'I will put this dog down tomorrow,' says the judge, removing his wig. He is almost bald underneath. The dog looks up at him, its crusted eye watering, running. It shivers in spasms, as though an electric current is pulsing through it.

'I wonder if it is chitterlings today,' says the barrel-chested man. He belches.

Were it possible to just eat, were it possible to just have sustenance, you would stay. As it is, there are far too many demands made on one in this place.

The light will keep changing. Were it possible to forget this feeling you have, this sense of revulsion such as you get when you lift a heavy stone that has been embedded in the earth for years, uncovering the walkways and meeting-places of small, dark creatures that may feast on corpses, you might find peace. But it is not here.

So, with a little reluctance, you get up; you leave a few coins for the waiter by way of thanks, and leave.

As you pull the door closed behind you, you hear the thin man call out to you, 'Mind. Aim straight for the heart. It is quicker that way.'

Ed's Theory of the Soul

Ed is on a beach, alone. He's left his clothes scattered on the larger rocks at the base of the cliff, back there. Started to fold them, then stopped, the ocean pulling him round like a magnet, passing on the tug of the moon. Ed knows the tide has something to do with the moon. But not the how or the why, just that it has.

He stops at the water's edge. Maybe it is alive. Like mercury, all of a piece, finding itself if it divides. Maybe the movement – a gentle pulse now – is really the sea breathing like everything must, if it lives. There's nothing more beautiful, so it must live. And if the ocean lives, does it feel?

Ed read a few weeks back, somewhere, can't remember, about a woman who loved a wall. A wall. That is amazing. There was a photo, too. She looked perfectly ordinary, standing next to this crumbling wall, glowering at the camera like it was intruding. Then a second shot. She'd turned away, maybe thinking the photographer had finished – and was stretching out a hand towards the wall. She was leaning in, her whole body following the hand, her eyes lowered, the fingers flexed, electric. Something in the ether reaching out from those fingertips, reaching out to the wall, and reaching out through the photograph to Ed – and the wall sending back something – something – Ed couldn't fathom it because he doesn't quite … but it was there. Ed felt it.

The wall cared.

But this? The water? Ed dips a foot in, the ankle still marked where his sock was tight. The water doesn't care. It's cold. Very cold. So cold the foot begins to hurt.

Ed sits on the pebbles, keeps his foot in the water, waits for it to stop hurting. Doesn't need to look round, see if anyone's watching. There is no-one. Ten miles to the nearest town, signs a couple of miles along the main road – Road Closed At Benacre. More signs if you do turn down past Monks' Farm and the abandoned church – No Entry. Cliff Edge Unstable. And the final signs up on the cliff top, where the road stops, sliced, layers of tarmac and hardcore exposed, like those things you should keep covered.

Danger, subsidence.

His body's not good, now. Used to be. Used to be hard, firm as a statue. Ed's foot is numb, the cold-ache travelling up his leg.

There was something in the local paper about the church, about Monks' Farm. But like the article about the woman and the wall, Ed can't quite remember it all. Something about the monks taking a tenth of their produce and burying it. Even in the depths of winter, when the stuff was really needed – buried for God. For God, for God's sake. Like God lives under the ground and is going to tunnel to find the stuff, and sit there consuming potatoes, carrots, cabbages, herbs, and turnips?

In the dark? Alone?

Ed sits with his foot in the sea and shakes his head. Wasn't it just the same thing? Like the woman and the wall? The monks knowing the very earth felt things, knew things? The monks feeding it? Ed can see them, if he shuts his eyes, and just listens to the sea's heartbeat. Sees the monks in a line, two abreast, in brown. Wicker trays of some sort, baskets. And their cheekbones throwing shadows down their faces. Their brows looming over lowered eyes. Carrying the goods to the churchyard to be buried. Ed will not open his eyes in case the vision fades. Strains his ears beyond the rush of the sea to hear the monks' plainchant.

But that's just imagining, nothing real, a silence in the past for the monks, broken only by the regular sounds of a horse clopping past on the lane, its hooves on the cold ground sounding like a knell. He hears that and feels a swell of something in his chest.

This morning, early, he took a woman to a town and saw her onto a train, and she left. This woman has a name, but Ed doesn't want to think about that. He stood on the platform, the train pulled out of the station, and something in him made him raise a hand, as though he was waving. Like the other woman with the wall. But he wasn't – it was only reflex, and he turned away and drove here.

Ed sits on the pebbles, one foot in the water. His eyes snapped open a moment ago, when the monks got to the place they needed, and tipped the goods into the ground. The horse had gone past with its cart, and all he could hear now was the sound of the monks' breathing, and their hearts beating, and the rattle and jolt of the cart fading up the lane. Like a film, that's all it was. That's where it all came from, his head. Seen it somewhere, must have, on the box, on the screen, not making it up at all, not inventing anything. His head full of other people's images – dragons and mountains, and rockets, plumed horses, jousting knights, stables, tin baths, mines and golden dishes on some distant planet's feast day.

She'd said to him, his woman, that he was hopeless. Treated her like an object, she said, and she was right – Ed loves them all, why should she be different to the rest? But she left. He won't even think of her name, and anyway, the sound of the sea becomes the sound of the train becomes the sound of the monks, the horse, the cart and the sea again.

As far as he can see, the sea. Right to the horizon – or where the horizon must be – you just have to trust, sometimes. Today, it is the same colour as the sea, the sky. It's all one.

Then, by Ed's foot, knocking into it, tapping against his skin, his anklebone, a something … not sea. Something small, a piece of wood. And Ed's scrabbling in the edge of the water to fetch the thing, a small stick, a piece. Light wood that floats without sinking at all. Can't remember what it's called. Used to use the stuff in models, making planes, with his dad, when he was a lad…

And in that single piece of wood, the world disappears and comes back. It leaves a black hole into which Ed can pour everything – how he can't remember what he's read, and where, and maybe he is hopeless, and stupid, and how the photo of that woman by the wall reached out to him, and how there is a soul in the smallest thing, even the stones he is kneeling on, his skin denting with the shapes under his bones.

There is a soul in the water, in the tiny drops that separate themselves from the edge of the sea, splitting over the pebbles. Soul in the pebbles. Ed is wide-eyed at the simplicity of this truth.

He stands, holding the piece of wood. The wood that came from somewhere out there – and he points it towards the horizon – and it is as though the wood remembers the cold, and settles back into his hand, digging into his palm as he grips it tighter, tighter. As though the wood wants to bury itself into his flesh, deeper, deeper, so that when Ed wants it, this feeling, he will have to dig.

And he wonders what that woman in the photo did about the wall. That thing streaming from her fingers was love. How Ed remembers it. How it streamed out of the photograph straight to him, too.

It's the same now, this piece of wood, wood that is not wood at all, and he is digging in his memory – to find his young fingers on another small piece of wood, at home, on the kitchen table, making something with his father. Then his father opening a blade, a blade that caught the light, and he went to bring it down on the piece of wood to make, what? A wing of a plane, or a house for a train set? Ed couldn't bear it – 'No!' and slid his hand across the table, between the wood and the blade.

Ed remembers.

Ed remembers, but doesn't need to. On his palm, wet with sea water, the mark where the point of the blade just pierced the skin, parting the tendons as it came through from the back of his hand, pinning him to the tabletop. And there was something that stopped the world then, the boy pinned to the wood by a blade, his father standing, mute, the air in the kitchen electric. As if it could be the end of something.

Ed turns his hand over to see the bigger scar on the back of his hand where the blade entered. The sea frothing over his knees like snow.

What was the woman's name, this morning? What is a name anyway? A sound we make, learned to make, something that sets one thing apart from another. How do we know the name is what the thing would choose for itself?

And what is living and dead? What is animal, vegetable, mineral? Who is to say that the sea cannot feel? Or a wall?

He saw the woman onto a train, in a town. He waited, on the platform, his hand raised, because his hand raised itself. He walked to the gates, standing to one side to let others onto the platform, because they always come, and move, and want to get from one place to another, and shift, and never stay the same.

He went to go home. To his home town. But what was that? A mass of roads, buildings, sewers running beneath them like veins under the skin. Alleys, fences, gateways and tall locked doors.

Walls.

And maybe, just maybe, the things we build have feelings. Maybe, just maybe, the woman with the wall is right. The wall feels, and yearns, and loves her in return. The thing he read said some women marry houses. And another, she married a bridge, and another a great steel tower…

Ed gets up. He carries the piece of wood back to the base of the cliff, rests it on a fallen rock while he dresses. And on his way back up the lane, he'll pause at the church, may walk for a while among the graves, the tumble of gravestones, all illegible now, covered in lichen. And he'll carry the piece of wood home, light as a bride, thinking that everyone dies, that over there won't be any different to here.

The cliff edge will crumble again in the high night tide, and blocks of tarmac, hardcore, will tumble to the beach in great blocks, layered, like chunks of wedding cake.

Taxi

Frank Merriman dropped a fare at The Grand then drove slowly back to the station. The 8.51 would arrive in ten minutes or so – still plenty to do. His head ached. He'd been working most of the night – the usual, pubs then clubs. He'd been caught for a fool again – picked up a giggling young couple at three in the morning, drove them all the way to Worthing into a maze of one-way residential streets he didn't know at all, and they upped and ran off without paying, leaving the doors wide open. Can't trust anyone these days. One more trip and he'd go home. He joined the line of taxis inching forward – a lot of people coming off the train, joining the queue for cars. Good.

He saw her straight away. Something about her reminded him of his wife – not that he'd seen Margaret for years, but maybe she'd look a bit like this now? The woman struggled out of the station, weighed down by two old suitcases and a carpet bag, which she put down on the pavement near the taxi rank. She wore some sort of raincoat open over a dress. Greying hair, cut not too short. The sleeves of the raincoat were frayed, but the collar of the dress was crisp, white. Old shoes. The carpet bag at her feet had a broken zip, showing something inside – something faded and blue. Didn't look like she had much spare cash. Wouldn't be a long job, whoever got that one. Looked like a talker, too. He could hear her now: 'To West Hill Street? My son's. Not far – I can't walk with these bags. He'll be at work, but he leaves the key. Thought I'd treat myself…'

Leaves the key … If he got her, and she did say that, Frank'd have something to say. How stupid it was to leave keys outside houses. How she shouldn't go around telling people. How you can't trust anyone these days…

Frank watched her from his old black cab, way back in the queue of cars, waiting, idling, edging forward. No real reason for watching her – just she was different. Something about her that seemed lost, as if Brighton Station had jumped up at her out of nowhere and she was making sense of it all. She stood beside the queue, close to the wall, touching it, as if she would have liked to blend with the bricks. She did not join the queue, just waited, watching. Suspicious, really. He kept an eye. Pickpockets behaved like that, hanging about until people were used to them, then zap – and wallets were lifted. Gone.

The cars inched forward. The queue of people inched forward. They bent to speak to the drivers, and got into the cabs in ones and twos.

Then the woman seemed to wake up – she straightened her shoulders and joined the back of the line. Frank saw her watching the cars closely as they pulled up beside the remaining fares, bending to see inside, peering at the drivers. He counted ahead. She wouldn't be Frank's fare though. She'd have the car in front. They could put up with her chatter, for two minutes to West Hill Street or wherever.

Thing was, he'd only ever tried to look after Margaret. And how could he look after her if he didn't know where she was, what she was up to? 'So where are you off to now? Who with? When will you be back?' It was the only thing they quarrelled about. 'The pub? With the girls? Jessie's birthday? Really?? Are you sure there isn't another man?' She'd said he was crowding her out and didn't trust her and that was no basis for a marriage. She didn't even take her hairbrush.

Frank sighed. Twenty five years back now. At least no children to worry about.

The car in front pulled up beside the woman. The new Mondeo, bright and brash, younger driver, loud music spilling from the dash, and the woman stood back, smiled, and waved another fare on instead. She peered at Frank's old black cab, at Frank, looking directly into his face until he had to look away. She paused, then dragged her cases to the kerb and waited for him to help her with her bags. She didn't say anything, just climbed in and waited while he shut the door behind her. Lady Muck down on her luck – Frank knew that sort too. Tight as ticks. Never give tips.

She chose to sit right in the corner. She arranged her carpet bag at her side like an armrest, then leaned back and closed her eyes. Like that, she didn't look like Margaret any more. Just worn out. Nice face though. Frank waited, the engine idling. When nothing was forthcoming he slapped back the glass partition. 'Where to?' he said, half-turning his head.

The woman looked up. 'Anywhere.'

Frank's headache was worse. This job, then he'd go home, get some sleep. 'C'mon, lady. I don't have all day.'

' I mean it. Anywhere,' the woman said again. 'I don't mind.' Her voice was soft. Educated. Maybe one of those educated con-women. Frank peered at her in his rear view mirror; he wasn't born yesterday, best call her bluff straight away. 'You got money for the fare?'

'Enough,' the woman said, closing her eyes again.

'You really mean "just drive"?'

She did not open her eyes. Just nodded.

Frank pulled away from the kerb. 'I've been waiting years for a fare to say that,' he said, the words coming from nowhere. He glanced in his rear view, expecting her to smile, but she did not.

The day was misty – a sea fret. Frank turned on his radio – a bit of classical, Beethoven, good for the nerves. He kept the wipers on intermittent. Every now and again, he glanced up at his mirror and occasionally he cleared his throat, but the woman did not respond. Her head, not altogether grey, rested against the back of the seat, but she did not look comfortable.

Frank drove his cab through the city, talking the main thoroughfares, joining the ebb and flow. He idled at traffic lights and stayed behind other vehicles that went slowly, indicators on, their drivers peering at street signs. No need to pass. No need to rush.

When he checked his mirror, he checked his passenger. Her eyes were still closed; her shoulders had relaxed now. The collar of the raincoat had fallen open, showing her neck. She was older than he thought. He smiled – weren't they all? Himself, too? He shook his head – his headache had gone – and he hadn't even felt it going. But he was going to need breakfast if he was going to drive around for much longer, no matter how slowly.

The next set of lights was outside a school. A young mother, struggling with a pushchair holding a toddler, was dragging a little boy along by the hand, a little lad who was pulling away from her, trying to get his hand out of her grasp – their voices fighting with the Beethoven...

'Thomas – will you come ON? You're late enough as it is. Don't be such a baby!'

'I hate you! I won't! I don't want to! I'm going to run away from you!'

...until Frank wound his window down, 'Hey – you be nice to your mum, Sonny. Mums are precious...' and

43

he grinned at the young mum, but she didn't grin back – too full of the day perhaps – but then maybe it was the music and no breakfast, but Frank is back, years back, with his own mum, and she's tucking him up, saying she's off out, and there's no time for a story tonight, but she'll read two tomorrow to make up, promise. And she's kissing him, and he can smell a new perfume, and it's lovely, and she's soft and special, and she's got on a new dress, which swishes, and he hears her go downstairs, and then the front door clicks. And he doesn't want to remember any more because when he comes downstairs in the morning, he finds his dad red-eyed in the kitchen saying, 'What time is school, Frankie? What do you have for breakfast, Frankie?' And for weeks he waits and waits and there is no Mum ever ever again … but she promised. She promised.

The blare of a horn – a shout, 'Colour blind are we?' and Frank, red-faced, put the cab into gear and moved off.

Later, on the outskirts of the city, he pulled into a petrol station with a café alongside. The woman lifted her head.

'Diesel,' Frank said. 'And I need a coffee. You?'

The woman said nothing. Frank shrugged, got out, stretched, filled up with diesel and queued to pay, keeping one eye on his cab. The woman didn't move. Then he drove round the side of the building and parked right by the café window. He left the keys in the ignition and started to walk towards the doors, but had a vision of the woman jerking awake, flinging open the doors, jumping into his seat and driving away with his cab. He returned, leaned in through the open window, pulled the keys out of the ignition and put them in his pocket. She was watching him.

'Back in ten,' he said.

The café was empty, apart from a waitress and the checkout girl talking by the till. The waitress was a young thing, foreign, thin, who brought him the cup of coffee and buttered toast he ordered, and did not look him in the eye.

From his table in the café he could see his cab. His passenger did not get out, even to stretch her legs. At one point she bent to her bags, then sat back, eyes downcast as though she was reading, but he could not quite see.

Frank finished his coffee, and called over that he would like another. The thin waitress looked up from her conversation at the till, and there was a pause before she brought over the coffee pot and a clean cup. And without asking whether it was what he wanted, she poured the coffee into this clean cup, turned away and returned to her conversation without clearing away the first.

The empty cup bothered him, and he pushed it away. It sat across the table as though someone had just finished it and got up. It was a long time since he'd sat at a table with two cups. Two plates. Two anything. Maybe he just wasn't meant to be one of two. Maybe he was meant to be just him. Maybe…

He went to the gents, and while he was there he splashed his face and ran wet fingers through his hair. Then he went to pay. Near the till were some shelves stacked with maps, bottles of water, packets of sweets – small green and white mints Margaret used to love.

Back in his cab, he started the engine. He slid the glass partition open and offered the woman a bottle of water over his shoulder.

'I thought…'

The woman paused then reached for the bottle. 'Thank you.'

'Do you like these?' Frank said, turning round, offering her the mints, and she shook her head, but thanked him again. For some reason, he thanked her back.

As Frank left the garage forecourt, he glanced one more in his rear view mirror. Before, she might have been reading. But now, she was leaning back in the corner of his cab and tucked behind her head was a large faded blue cushion.

'Make yourself at home,' Frank said, and it felt the right thing to say. Just as not trusting her earlier, the keys – stuck in his mind now, and niggled at him, like a splinter.

For a while, he drove his cab in silence. When the city was well behind them, he spoke.

'You awake?'

'Yes,' she said.

'I'm sorry,' he said, watching her in the mirror. 'I'm sorry I took the keys.'

There was a pause. She smiled. 'There was no need,' she said. 'No need at all. Your car is quite safe with me.'

For a moment, she sat there, watching the hedgerows the fields, the church spire of a village over to the left. Then she leaned forward.

'In case…' she stopped, and started again. 'In case you were worried – I do have money to pay you for this journey,' she said. 'Look…' and she was dragging the carpet bag onto her knee, searching inside.

This time, Frank didn't answer. He just shook his head, relaxed his hands on the wheel and as though he was sharing a secret, something too new to speak of yet, his voice fell to almost a whisper.

'I believe you,' he said. 'No need to show me.' He drove on for a while, feeling lighter than he had for a long time, before he met her eyes in the rear view mirror.

'I thought we might go north,' he said.

Housekeeping

At Victoria Station, she only just catches the train – whistles shrilling, people milling – her heart-rate high, higher. The train is packed, not a seat to be had, but no matter. She stands near the doors, pushes her overnight bag against a partition and leans. She gives herself up to the movement of the train, tucks her hair behind her ears like a teenager, although it's a long time since she was, and her mother used to say, 'Must cut your hair, Patty, too long,' and instead of a trip to the hairdresser's like everyone, everyone else, out would come the kitchen scissors.

Patty shakes her head, looks round to see if – but nobody is paying attention. She touches her fringe, new, cut straight across – she did that herself, last night, dropped the brown strands into the pedal bin. Mother would not have allowed that.

Will he like her fringe? When he sees her. And what will he say? What will she say to him, for that matter?

After a while, when her heart has stopped crowding out her thoughts, she is pushing her way down the train with her bag, 'Sorry, may I just? Thank you,' until she finds him. Her Mr Owen. Her Mr Professor Owen.

There he is, in the next carriage, only a few seats away, hunched over his papers, his back to her. The grey-brown curls, the back of his neck. Blue shirt. She ironed that for him only three days ago. There's no table. He's balancing the papers on his briefcase. Perfect. He will see her when she sits down, when a seat is free. All of her. She will sit, put her overnight bag on her knee and fold her coat on top. Her legs will be quite visible, and when Mr Professor Owen looks up, as he will, he will see that one of her legs is bare. Quite, quite naked. The other is nicely covered – a stocking, sensible and brown. Both legs end in equally sensible brown shoes for travelling. She will enjoy watching his face then – oh, she will! One naked leg indeed!

'Oh, Mr Owen,' she will say, when she finds the courage. 'I only just made it. I stopped in the Ladies' Room – and had to run to catch the train … but in the end I found you. Mr Owen, I found you.'

Not used to running. Not as young as she was.

But before she can do any of that she must stand here by some different doors and wait, wait until someone gets off, and then she can sit down where she can see him, clearly. And he will see her. He will look up, questioning. He will look down at her bare leg, back up to her face. She might nod – nonchalantly, she's been practising this – and say, 'Ah, I have been on the same train as you ever since you left Pontypool – making sure you didn't catch sight of me.'

What will he say, Mr Owen – actually Professor Owen, but he does not use that name much – when he catches sight of his housekeeper here on the train to Brighton? With one bare leg… 'Well, well,' he might say. 'Patty Evans, is that you? You are a long way from home, Patty. A long way from Pontypool. How come?'

Patty may say something about it being a fine time to travel, and she has heard Brighton is a fine place to visit.

Mr Professor Owen may explain he is going to a scientific conference and must give a speech too – but Patty knows all that already. She has read all the correspondence in his study back home. Oh, she does go in… 'I do, Mr Owen, even though you told me I must not clean in there.'

You see, lately, Mr Professor Owen, Patty Evans, your housekeeper, has been taking off her clothes as she works in your house. It was not easy to do at first, but it has become easier and easier. She has been leaving things – a blue floral blouse, for example, or a paisley scarf, where you might easily find them and, so far, he has not noticed. That gives her great pleasure. It is as though her things and Patty Evans herself are finding a home, as if yours is the house where Patty Evans has been born again.

Always, Mr Professor Owen, Patty Evans has left her shoes outside your front door. Not for their dirt on your floor, Mr Owen, for they would be unlikely to leave a trace – she would wipe them until they shone, until you could inspect her thinning soles as closely as you liked with the microscope in your study, and not find a single germ. No – she leaves off her shoes so her feet might be where yours have walked. She has heard from her cousin, the electrician, how you sometimes pace the rooms barefoot when you are working. From the very beginning, she liked to feel through her stockinged feet all your surfaces – the flagstones in the hallway, the polished boards in the study, the rug by the grate where your feet have stood and helped you think while you planned your experiments for the laboratory in Monmouth.

But will you remember who she is, when she sits down? She hopes so. She may need to say, 'You and I have only met the once, Mr Owen, when I came for interview.' And she may need to remind you what she said that day, 'I am a spinster. I live with my mother. I mean, I lived with my mother. For a long time. But now – she is gone.' You told her that it was admirable, caring for an elderly parent –

and – after only a few questions – gave Patty Evans the job of housekeeper.

Mr Professor Owen – she was admirable in your eyes. You said so. That was, and is, marvellous.

You leave her notes, to give her direction, such as, 'Please clean the kitchen today, Patty, and sweep the outside passageway,' 'The bathroom could do with a going over, please tidy the airing cupboard,' and 'Patty – don't touch my study again.'

Since that last she does still go in to your study, but never touches anything, not even to dust. She almost fears it as much as loves it; it has become a room where your echo is like a heavy beat at its centre.

Each time Patty comes to clean your house, she stares at the photographs on your desk, on the cabinet – there are so many of you as a student, with other students, in gowns and caps. One in particular she has grown to be very fond of – you on graduation day, she presumes, holding a scroll, a brightly coloured hood attached to your academic gown – and next to you, a woman. Who is she? She loves you, that much is plain – the way she is leaning in to you, comfortable with your body, as if it, and you, were a shield against something unseen. Patty Evans recognises that, but has never … at least not until now. There is no woman living with you. You should have a woman.

Patty knows where you are staying for your three-day scientific conference – at that great white hotel right on the seafront. She looked at the hotel brochure, on your desk. Like a wedding cake, that hotel. A great big wedding cake. Patty will be staying with another cousin, who has lived in Brighton for years. His wife works at the very hotel you are staying at – isn't that marvellous? She is a housekeeper too. Patty will no doubt persuade her to let Patty into your room … and oh, what fun she will have. She has yet to decide what items of clothing she will secrete around the room, but, oh, she will, she will. This bare leg is just a start.

She has the stocking in her pocket. If she can push it into your own pocket as she passes, she will.

Patty Evans is such a creature of habit. Once, you did not leave the keys for her, as you usually do, and she stood outside the house for what must have been ten minutes, close to tears. But then she saw that the bedroom window was ajar. She went to the passageway and managed to get the double ladder down from its clips on the wall, and she climbed in to your bedroom like a thief.

The bedroom, your bedroom, when she climbed in that day, was where it started. Patty snagged her brown cardigan on the windowframe. There was a piece of rough metal, and it caught at her sleeve as she jumped down, and suddenly, there she was, in her stockinged feet in your bedroom, quite breathless from the effort of climbing. She took off that cardigan … but your bed, Mr Professor Owen. Your double bed. Unmade. Both pillows dented, the blankets that covered you, and the sheet, all thrown back, trailing on the floor. Who…?

Patty Evans picked up a pillow and breathed in its scents. She had done that before, many times. Not you. Not you. She knows your smell, you smell strong, but good; your scalp sometimes leaves the scent of old wood, or sacking, or tar, she can't describe it well. No – this was something else, someone else, lighter, the slopes of that pillow were slicked with something sweet she could detect and did not like. The other pillow was yours – you had been lying on the side nearest the window, when normally you lie on the other.

Patty Evans, too, lay on your bed, Mr Professor Owen. She felt every inch of it. She tore off the sheet, and buried her face in it, here, there, this side, that – breathing in where your hands, and feet, and your whole body had lain. And the other one as well. Another man's wife? There has been talk of a woman; Patty Evans does not like that.

Why? Because she is a woman too. She is getting older.

It was cold, suddenly, in your bedroom. Patty pulled the window shut, and went to put her cardigan back on – with the wool unravelling, the stitches in loose loops as though they were clutching for each other – help, don't let me go, reach me, try, try harder … but there were too many eyes, the photographs, you and you and you and you, watching what she was doing. She turned them to face the wall, and while no-one, not even you, was watching, she stripped the bed, and before she remade it, slipped that brown cardigan beneath the mattress cover. She even left you a note to say it was missing, asked if you had seen it. You left her one in return, 'No cardigan reported…'

Now, Patty Evans is all over your house. Each time she is there, she removes her clothes. Last week, she took off her blouse, green and high-necked, a handkerchief still in the pocket – and draped it over the chair by the kitchen table. This skirt she is wearing now, so sensible, brown tweed and baggy with a kick-pleat she has never managed to iron flat – that has been laying on the flagstones in your hallway. And Patty has carried on cleaning, without them.

She is becoming bolder. You have changed her, Mr Professor Owen. Before, she might have kept both blouse and skirt with her, in the room she was tidying, just in case you came home unexpectedly. Now … she is different. You have made her daring. She walks through your house in her underwear, and most days, it feels quite warm. Upstairs, in your bedroom, she removes her stockings, one by one, pointing her toes as she saw someone doing once, in a film. And she fetches a chair and ties them both to the curtain rail. There! Things are always so scattered – impossible to dress quickly, if you reappear, Mr Professor Owen.

She even opened the windows and called when Miss Darking, the spinster next door, walked past on her way to the shops. Miss Darking saw Patty at the window in her petticoat. Her petticoat! It has lace. It is a good one. It does not match the brassière, which, in turn, does not match the other things … Patty has never afforded a set. Her mother would not allow … but her mother is gone, and now she is joining you in Brighton!

She has plans. When you both have your weekend in Brighton, you at your conference, and Patty at her cousin's two streets from the seafront, Patty shall visit your hotel bedroom over and over – and perhaps she will leave her brassière over your bedside light. Oh, it will look well. She took it off once at your house, and draped it over your microscope, in the study, and stood there in just … and it felt so … exciting! She will do it again, as soon as she gets back. But here, in Brighton, she is even more liberated – and who knows what she will get up to in your room? Afraid, and hoping, hoping and afraid, that you will return.

You see, Mr Professor Owen, Patty has already started, by removing her stocking. And look! The train is slowing, and the gentleman opposite you is putting his newspaper in his briefcase, snapping it shut, reaching up to collect his coat from the rack. He is leaving and Patty Evans, your housekeeper, one leg bare just for you, is ready to sit down.

Parallax

I was only saying to Frances, the woman on the next machine, night shift, 'Think about it. If true North exists, and I'm not saying it does, then you'll come close to pointing in the right direction if you go straight to the end of the pier.' I walked my fingers up my outstretched arm to show her. 'It's slowly does it,' I said. 'One foot in front of the other, slowing everything down. Like you're only just realising you can stand upright. Oh, and you have to watch the horizon with both eyes.'

Frances pulled the plug on the injection moulding. Threatened to go to the Supervisor. Said I was harassing her. Typical bloke, apparently.

'Look,' I said. 'The pier points to true North. That's all I'm saying.'

Frances asked to be moved to the Amtec room, so they moved her. Brought in this man off the replacement list from the agency instead. Georg something, from Romania. Pronounced Gay-Org. He just got on with the job and no talking back, smoked roll-ups in tea-breaks, two moles on his left cheek and that's about it. He was no-one. Inasmuch as anyone can be no-one.

That night, after a couple of weeks, we were conversing like old mates. Or rather, I was conversing, he was listening. Three a.m. tea-break, just him and me on the shift, us and the hiss of the hydraulics, like something breathing beneath the factory. The Amtec room closed for re-tooling, so no Frances and the others making snide comments about true North.

I was explaining, to myself as much as anything, 'It's got to do with parallax. The way an object moves if you look at it from different angles. Only it doesn't.'

Georg stirred his tea, listening. My Romanian is limited. His English is worse. I looked over at him, 'Know what I'm on about?'

He smiled, put two more teaspoons of sugar in his mug. 'Parallax,' he said slowly.

'Exactly. Useful concept. You can measure the distances between stars that way. I think.'

He nodded.

The machines packed up at four-thirty. Power cut, I reckon, although they said later it was the fuses blowing all together, and the notice they posted the next day talked about going for compensation from Grant Bros. But, for now, we'd have to take two weeks off, quarter pay. Georg looked at the notice (hasty photocopy, four typos) and he said the most complete sentence I'd heard yet, 'This very difficult.'

'You're telling me, mate,' I said.

Then he said the thing that made me invite him to stay for those weeks off. 'This very difficult, like parallax.'

It turned out he was taking about rent. Or the lack of it. Some place down by the docks, one of those illegal hostels, six to a room, mattresses on the floor.

In the car, he pointed to the speedo. Grinned.

'Of course, yup,' I said, and he was right. 30 mph to me in the driving seat was 35 mph to him in the passenger seat. The needle moved. Or didn't.

Georg didn't mind the state of my place. Since Helen went, I don't do much clearing up, but I do like my reading. Kid's enyclopaedias. Get them really cheap these days, out of date before they're printed. Georg picked a few up, put them in a pile, patted it.

He wouldn't bother me, just for a week.

After a couple of days we did go a bit stir-crazy. You can't just say 'parallax' endlessly, and smile and bob and look through your fingers at things on the wall moving relative to a chair on the rug between you and them. So, the third day, we went out. We walked on the prom, then on the pier, and I pointed out to sea and said, 'True North?' and Georg smiled and pulled his collar up. We walked round the lake, round the town centre – didn't have a lot of spending money, so not much we could do. I pointed to the edge of town, to where you can see the start of the hills, and the pylons. I said, 'Up there?'

He nodded, wisely. 'Up there.'

Up to the hill, to the hangar woods. There was enough petrol in the car for a few miles. Hadn't been there since goodness knows when – good place to walk, do some bird-watching maybe.

They must have changed the roads since I last came up here. What I thought was the right road became a lane, and the lane petered out at a farm gate. We reversed, ready to try again. I could see the ridge above us. Georg pointed at the trees, old trees up there on the skyline, rows of them, dying mostly, birches I think.

'You get those in Romania?' I said.

He just echoed, 'Romania…'

I always thought Helen and I would end up living in a village, somewhere small, pretty, hills, woodland. Fields. Here we were, Georg and I, sitting in the car on the escarpment, above plenty of villages, those trees lined up over our heads. Roots lifting out of the earth, like they were reaching for something.

I don't know what time we set out, after the walk on the prom, the pier, round the town, but it wasn't that light. Georg took out his roll-up tin, looked over. 'You mind?' I said I didn't, it was fine to smoke.

The lane was narrow, overhung with trees. Not that easy to reverse round those corners, the banks far too close. Georg had stretched back in his seat, head back, looking out of the window, up, up at the ridge over our heads. Down below, lights were coming on in the houses. The sky between the trees was grey, the branches and trunks like black things drawn against the evening. He'd lit up, the car was smoky. Made the trees blur, the patches of sky grow and blossom like there were angels waiting in the treeline. I was backing the car slowly, very slowly.

Georg leaned forward, tapped the speedo. 'No miles.'

We'd almost stopped. 'If we're going backwards, I suppose the mileage undoes itself?' I said, and then there was a sound, the evening coming into the car, cool, and Georg had got out into the lane. Through a gap in the hedge, between the trees. Gone. Up there, I saw him, crossing the last bit of escarpment, climbing towards the ridge in his cheap gym shoes. Thin jacket flapping. Gone.

I'd like to say I smelled something, perhaps. Something different, spicy, heady. But I didn't. Just his cigarette smoke thinning with the open door, the air. I'd like to say I heard something – a stone turned beneath a shoe, the rush of last year's leaves, whatever noise the sky makes when it turns from grey to greyer. Or a rook leaving a dying birch tree on a ridge.

I waited. Three days into a week off, and you're open to things. More awake. The same as when Helen left. I waited.

When it was really dark, I turned the car in a gateway and freewheeled down the hill to the village. To the pub. Ordered a pint, and a steak. Didn't worry about how I was going to pay. There weren't that many people in there. A couple in the corner drinking glasses of wine. A youngster throwing darts. And the bloke behind the bar, thin mousy hair, foreign accent, like Georg's. He could have been Georg – they all look alike, high cheekbones, grey eyes – only, of course, he couldn't have been.

There was a sound then. The woman in the corner running her finger round and round the rim of her wineglass. My plate was empty. My pint. The lights of a car reflected in the window, white light, red light. White light. Red. I moved my head from side to side, the light changing colour depending on how you looked at it. From here. Or there. And the wineglass went on singing until I wasn't sure it was the glass at all.

Captain Quantum's Universal Entertainment

an expanding story, with no boundaries

Your Most Qualified Guide to the Fairground (he has the badges to prove it) will not stop talking.

'Watch where you tread,' he says, 'those shoes look expensive. These elephants, you know how it is, what goes in must come out. The children feed them all sorts of unsuitable things: cherry buns, toffee apples, spun sugar.'

He tells you the Fairground is doing rather well these days. Says that it, like this story, is expanding apace, new side-shows every other day. He gives figures, but you are not listening. He smiles, pulls you into the sudden darkness between two tents, skirts a low edifice from which animal sounds and smells emerge, dives behind a caravan, side-stepping something indefinable which smells rank, but he does not seem to worry. He flings his head back, inhales, sighs. 'Smell the oil lamps, the crowd, the sawdust and mud, scalding chestnuts, the mechanical and the only-too-alive horses. I love this place, but I sometimes think mechanical is better, don't you agree?'

You are about to say that no, flesh and blood are best – but he does not wait for your answer. Maybe he does not believe journalists have valid opinions on the natural state of things.

'Adjust your eyes to the eternal Fairground night,' he demands. (You adjust them.) 'Appreciate, if you will, our flaming torches in their iron braziers.' (You appreciate them.) 'How expansive light is! Oh, this throng – how they push!'

On and on, as if you are blind and have lost your sense of smell. You most certainly have not. Your forthcoming article for the *Biennial Journal of Theoretical Prognostication* will be the better for a few smells. Ah. Let him talk. He is writing your article for you. You reach into your top pocket, press your finger to the Patent Bodyheat-Control Recording Device.

'Look at those sideshows,' he says, skipping further and further into the Fairground. (You look.) 'Candy stripes in all colours, no expense spared here. Bunting flying high, top-hatted showmen and scuttling dwarves, our ubiquitous monkeys' bow-legged backflips. They do not like their chains. Would you?' (You would not.) 'Oh, look, look over there, the field lit by more torches? Watch…'

And you do, and catch your first glimpse of the Silver Flight Machine with its great wings, its coal turbines and what must be back-up gas canisters at its sides. You want to stay, see it more, let the P B-C Recording Device take notes, but an engine passes and your Guide is off again.

'Ah! The traction engine – do you feel its heat on your face?' (You do.) 'Do your ears ring as you taste its oil and soot on your tongue?' (They do.) 'Here – a mint humbug perhaps, to take away the oil?'

You do not like mint humbugs, but the taste is better than oil. And you almost choke as he tugs your arm again – and this time, maybe this time he will lead you to what you are here for, the two great stars of the Fairground among the ever-expanding constellations of lesser ones. The Great Maximilian, jongleur extraordinaire, and Lucille, the Incredible Shrinking Bearded Lady. You pat your pocket again; yes, still there with the recorder, the notebooks containing research you have memorised (you have entitled the research 'Ruminations'), and the questions you must ask when you are face-to-face with history. If such is possible.

Your Guide again, 'Quick, come with me. Let us pause in these shadows; and look, see who comes through the crowd! Oh, my goodness – the Ringmaster. Does your story have room?' What a question! You assure him your story has no edges. But then...

Your heart does a chained-monkey backflip. Captain Quantum himself – oh – the great, the one and only – but all is not well. For heaven's sake. This is precisely why you are here, this is why *The Biennial Journal* booked you this Most Qualified Guide to the Fairground, promising he was the best, not mentioning he was also the most voluble.

He sees you are distracted, pulls your sleeve, his own face a mirror of sudden dejection – such an actor, with an actor's clear diction! 'Notice,' he says, 'notice how the Captain drags his feet, for all the polish of those black boots?' (You notice.) 'Notice how he brushes his top hat on his sleeve, the half-apologetic glances to the left and right. Do you see the slight droop of the head, the effort to keep the shoulders strong in their almost-well-cut scarlet but stained tailcoat?' (You do see.) 'Do you see, unshaven-chinned as he is, that half-waxed and uneven moustache?' (Oh shut up. You see.) 'Usually so dapper, so polished. Captain Quantum himself. It doesn't matter how often you see him; he binds, spell-like – do you not find?' (You do find, reluctantly.) 'Certainly one for the ladies in his time. And his time, ah, his time – perhaps it wanes, like the sun when the earth turns its back on her, flexes?'

You have no idea what your Guide is talking about, if

you are honest, but you smile nevertheless. And he smiles back, delighted to be of service, and vanishes.

You may shrug. Who needs Most Qualified Guides on a night like this? You carry on watching as Captain Quantum ascends the stage in front of his own tent, his own Big Top, his performance space. A hand to his mouth. A cough. Tosses back his greying curls, and straightens those shoulders. Your fingers reach for your Recording Device.

His voice – half what it once surely was. Gravel, dust, faded boot-black. 'Ladies and gentlemen. Have your smelling salts ready: your *sal volatile*, ladies, your spirit of hartshorn. Your dark, veiled hats – so attractive and mysterious, the very thing our greatest stars cannot resist – the one, Maximilian, such a man as has never … the other, Lucille, such a lady…'

And he turns aside, weeping. You must remember that. *The Journal* readers will love it, love it – but he is speaking again.

'My apologies. I forget myself. For one final time, you are invited to enter Captain Quantum's Universal Entertainment. Take your seats, please, for the Final Act, at no cost whatsoever. Completely free, other than time. Your time. Mine, theirs. For aeons, just for your delight, delectation, rapture and relish, Captain Quantum has laid before the discerning a veritable cornucopia of consanguineous delight. Everything has been in balance – tightrope walkers high above the sawdust, elephants on glittering cylinders. But tonight, ladies and gentlemen, ah, tonight. I beg your indulgence for a short moment, while the stars of this evening's performance – the final performance – ready themselves.'

It is almost time. The story progresses along its own path. Finally, you will see the man who has starred in Captain Quantum's Universal Entertainment for as long as memory's fingers stretch. And his chosen lady…

The crowd begins to grow, waiting to pile through the

canvas entrance tunnel. You hold back, remembering your research, details related by Fairground babblers who responded to your advertisement, keen to see their names credited in *The Biennial Journal*. Your 'Ruminations'.

Ruminations

The Great Maximilian. Background.

- Been around for aeons, apparently. (Past it?)
- Wears pink tights. White slippers. Silk shirt. (No taste.)
- Plate spinner par excellence. (Apparently.)
- Can keep one hundred plates spinning at once. (Unlikely.)
- He will attempt this feat in a final try to persuade his Chosen One to be his.
- Chosen One = Lucille, the Incredible Shrinking Bearded Lady. 100% natural beard (apparently), as grows on the chins of the best Chinese seers. (Wispy?)

But wait. Is the story going a little fast? Let's slow it down a little. Too slow? Then speed it up by all means. It is simple enough – this is a partnership, is it not? Everything is relative.

Look, the crowd still grows, waiting to enter the tent – you have time. Consider the mysterious Lucille. Back to your 'Ruminations'.

The Great Maximilian (TGM) and his multiplicities.

- TGM is a perfectly ordinary man. (But…)
- Multiple occupations. (Busy man.)
- Daily dress. Underneath layer: pink tights and white silk shirt. Then chinos and open neck shirt, or an ill-fitting grey suit. Then a workman's garb and thick boots. (Must be hot.)
- Layers peel off as the day progresses.
- In the mornings, TGM makes, builds, on a large scale. The Fairground itself is Maximilian's own creation,

(more or less). All the buildings, sideshows. Hawsers the span of a strongman's bicep. (Apparently.) Great airships, flying machines, steam-powered bridges (and the rest).

- Afternoons: off come the boots, on go a pair of suede lace-ups. TGM becomes a scientist. A Physicist, paid according to likelihood, likelihood defined by anonymous Committee. (To be verified.) Beavers away in the glow of gas-powered screens.
- Evenings – circus slippers. He becomes the Great Maximilian, renowned the Universe over for his spinning plates – the numbers of which are growing.

This story wordcount grows. But sadly, oh – sadly – The Great Maximilian's downfall is and was (all at once, for time folds, repeats, intermarries itself) and will be imminent. And it is all down to his weakness with women. Of course.

Back to your 'Ruminations'?
One week in The Love History of Maximilian (as related by Henrietta, his first love).
- Sunday: Maximilian fell in love at sixteen. Henrietta, daughter of the lion tamer. A few scratches, but not so's you'd notice, and all went well for at least a couple of days. By Tuesday he had taken her virginity and his own in a small caravan that smelled of bacon. (Bacon?)
- Wednesday: He saw Mandy. No scratches. Perfect. It was early in the morning, before she donned her trapeze kit, stretching her hamstrings against a closed-up spun-sugar stall.
- You can do a lot of things up against closed up spun-sugar stalls. (Indeed?)
- Still Wednesday: By teatime, Mandy was becoming predictable; Henrietta was old hat. And Lucille, the Incredible Shrinking Bearded Lady, was going for a trim.

(Lucille!) TGM waited for her outside the barber's, and wooed her with a smile. Lucille, freshly hot-towelled, smooth cheeked, neat goatee, was smitten, and French. Good day, that Wednesday. (But it would have Repercussions.)

- Thursday a.m.: he rested, first with Lucille, then with Mandy, lastly with Henrietta.
- Thursday afternoon: Captain Quantum's wife Maggie came to him as he practised balancing six sticks on his nose. Older, experienced, dangerous (not the sticks, Maggie). She taught him a lot.
- Thursday night, he excused himself from Maggie's pink nylon boudoir, and returned to Henrietta, via firstly Lucille and then Mandy.
- By Friday, he needed the company of a bloke, any bloke, went to the pub with Jungle Jimmy, the Mad Midget. Innumerable pints of strong ale. Women. Ruckus. He shut his ears to the ruckus, and bought four bunches of roses. Kept three in a bucket while he serviced Maggie. Two in the bucket while he apologised to Lucille, one in the bucket while he saw to Mandy. And he saved the biggest bunch for Henrietta, because there will never, ever, be anyone like the first. (So he said.)
- Saturday morning, The Amazing Marengos arrived. From Bulgaria. Thirteen identical sisters (three sets of triplets and a foursome) renowned for their skill on horseback.
- By Sunday (and he was only sixteen) he'd put a smile on the faces of Una, Dua, Tria, Quattria, Cinka, Sexia, Septua, Octavia, Nova, Decca (she became famous later in vinyl), Unadecca, Duadecca, Tridecca, Maggie, Lucille, Mandy … and of course reserved a special place in his heart for Henrietta. (Etc.)
- (Henrietta now happily married, and a grandmother.)

You are feeling tired. (You are.) However, you know

that a deeper understanding of the components leads to a more holistic view of the Fairground itself. And anyway the crowd is not yet in the tent. You must have patience.

You turn to the other star in the 'Ruminations'.
Lucille, the Incredible Shrinking Bearded Lady.

- Not TGM's first love, but the longest lasting. (Brave woman.)
- Puckish, mercurial, a past not dissimilar to Maximilian's but sufficiently different to maintain interest, as the story expands even further, and takes on her extraordinary shape-shifting potential, and your 'Ruminations' continue so deeply you don't notice the crowd beginning to enter the Big Top. Lucille and her multiplicities. (As related by Captain Quantum, her employer.)
- Saturdays: she is herself, the Incredible Shrinking Bearded Lady.
- She guarantees to finish each performance half the size she was when she began.
- She doubles her mass in the same time-frame. (Should be impossible, but is not, as proven by the best steam-powered calculators. (Apparently.)
- Sundays, she rests (as all good bearded ladies do?!)
- Mondays, she reappears as Natalia, the Tiny Bearded Knife Thrower. Small knives, but deadly.
- Knives ought to fly in straight lines, these do not. (Apparently.) Almost invisible blades hum their un-straight path across the ring, and disappear into a cork board behind Natalia's latest assistant. (Apparently, they are replaced with frightening regularity.)
- Tuesdays, she is Carmen. Has to be seen by each spectator through magnifying lenses. Balances on a spangled globe on one finger while playing a little something by Gustav Holst on the harmonica. (Through her beard?)
- Sometimes, it is recognisable as part of *The Planets* suite, but she says it showed such a lack of vision to leave

it there, that she has composed the rest of the Musical Universe herself. (? more research needed.)

- Wednesdays, she is Ingrid. Skates in an ice bubble, the top of which is never seen. Skates at such speed she never loses adhesion, no matter which way up she is travelling. The curvature is progressively covered in her trails until they cover it with a glistening web, until somehow (no-one has worked out how) she breaks free, ice shattering around her as she performs a faster and faster spin on a single fragment, becoming a blur, and finally disappearing, beard and all.
- Thursdays, she is Bertha and Briony, the miniature conjoined three-legged acrobat, completely double-jointed (of course!), facial hair knitting (most charmingly) with every effort.
- Friday, she is Pint-Sized Susie and the Littlest Schnauzers. She's trained them to count to infinity plus one.
- The schnauzers also 'speak' in nursery rhymes (their Twinkle Twinkle Little Star is unforgettable, apparently), and ride penny-farthings round the perimeter (while their mistress preens her chin?).

Perhaps you can hear the two of them, Maximilian and Lucille?

'Lucille, you Incredible Shrinking Bearded Lady, you – I want you, I need you…' Maximilian, whispering in her ever-tinier ear.

'You can have me, if you can find me…' her teasing reply as she nears her own vanishing point.

Without the Most Qualified Guide to chivvy, you have lagged behind the mass. You almost miss him (not quite!) – voluble and annoying as he was. Into the entrance tunnel, then, you leave the bright torches of the Fairground behind, exchanging the warmth of chestnuts, burning sugar, gas flames, for something grubby, old, dark, smelling of what – sawdust? Greasepaint? There is no-one else in the tunnel – maybe they have already gone through. You would ask your Most Qualified Guide, this tunnel seems too long, you thought it would be a matter of moments, but this? As if you have taken a wrong turning. You look back. Forward. You touch the walls, faded canvas, stained. Sacking on the ground, damp, uneven and clinging, round corner after corner. Is this really leading to the home of the Great Maximilian, jongleur extraordinaire, and Lucille, the Incredible Shrinking Bearded Lady?

The ceiling sags. You can reach up and touch it, covered as it is in half-hearted stars: tin, plastic perhaps, pinned at one or two points. A few have fallen. You check no-one is watching, bend, pick one up, put it in your pocket.

The scent of something animal now: fear, dung, fur, sweat – which seems to get stronger the further you walk? You make a mental note, an apology for the maltreatment of the universe, a clever sentence with which to start your article. But then, you arrive.

Captain Quantum's Big Top, the venue for the famous Universal Entertainment, is not full by any calculation. You make your way up a few wooden steps to a bench, sit in your own pool of light, two or three rows back in order to take in the atmosphere … but there is little. The ring is illuminated by just enough torches in rusting holders.

Beyond, around, the spectators, mostly singles, occasionally couples, even more occasionally family groups, sit separated from each other by patches of darkness that seem almost elementary, full of strange possibilities. Apart from the hiss of the steam-lamps, the occasional spark from the torches, whispers, there is no other sound – and, as for light, there is not enough to fill the space, just enough to point up the ring and its raked sawdust, the old wooden benches in gradually disappearing tiers away from the ring, unpainted tent poles leading up to nowhere, for it is too dark to see the roof. (You try.) Or the sides, for that matter. (You try.) As if the tent is boundless. Like the story.

And then. Curtains lift. A fanfare, ragged, but a fanfare still. A flight of white doves (white doves? Honestly…), which scatter across the ring into the darkness, a few feathers drifting, and Captain Quantum strides out into the centre of the ring. He says … nothing. His arms are raised – as if to embrace whoever comes next.

The Great Maximilian comes next. White tights, white slippers, spangled vest, amid a halo of flying trumpets that seem to touch his fingers hardly at all, flying in time to a beat set up by invisible drums. (This is what you expected.) A dwarf in an identical costume scuttles behind, dragging a white cart piled high with canes; a second and a third pull carts laden with white plates that rattle in their piles over the sawdust ridges. (Also expected.) In the torchlight, The Great Maximilian seems to shimmer as he juggles with his trumpets, playing a chromatic scale perfectly as each one brushes his lips as they pass. The spectators applaud, whistle, stand and shout. He tries harder, harder, doubling the number of trumpets, playing a duet with himself on flying instruments. (Amazing!)

A dwarf clambers up the steps, handing out magnifying scopes to either side. Through yours, once wiped, you can see the separate grains of sand in the ring, the footsteps left by The Great Maximilian's dance, dust raised from his frantic moves. The halo of the trumpets. The wheels of the waiting carts, cane and plate. You can see the man – his face, every pore – for all his make-up, he is drawn. His cheeks glow grey in the flickering torchlight as the drums do their thrumming. Louder, louder, a broken rhythm as he lets the trumpets fall, one by one, into the hands of a waiting dwarf.

He moves to stand between the carts. Mouths, 'For you, Lucille…' (You do wish he would not be quite so romantic). Takes a single cane. Holds it so lightly. A dwarf hands him a plate … and it starts.

He throws the first plate into the air, catches it atop a cane and sets it spinning. He repeats the action, over and over, until his left hand is a strange orbitless orrery with twenty, thirty attendant white planets and moons, each spinning at their own speeds. The dwarves move closer to help, until The Great Maximilian's right hand is a mirror of the left. The spectators shift on their benches, lean forward, trying to count. Is that forty, fifty or sixty? Someone shouts, 'Count them, count!' (Good idea.)

He does not waver. And they count. You hold your breath. '…seventy one, seventy two…' Moves his fingers to encourage a vacillating planet to straighten, resume its spin. '…eighty…' Keeps his eyes on all the canes, all the planets. '…eighty four, eighty five, eighty six…' until he bristles, plates spinning round him catching the torch-light like so many fireflies. Starts to turn himself, dance, canes between his teeth, '…ninety one…' his own spinning keeping the fireflies alive until he is a blur. No man this. And the dwarves keep throwing new plates into the mass, and they find their cane, and spin with the rest. '…ninety nine…'

But what of Lucille? Here is The Great Maximilian, performing for her like the best bird in the jungle, waiting for his mate. Then you see her. At least, probably. What you definitely see is Captain Quantum bowing to nothing you can see at all. (You tried. Several times).

The editor of *The Biennial Journal of Theoretical Prognostication* will reject your careful account of the spectacle that followed, suggesting you spend a little time on a retreat to gather your faculties. (The cheek.) You will read and re-read your submission to see what, if anything, was wrong.

(There isn't.) Whether facts were skewed – and will find nothing amiss. You will go on your retreat and return a little lighter, a little older. (They paid.)

Later, when it is all done, you will remember, while writing the article, you thought at first of a flea circus, such as you once saw in Torquay. The only indication that the flea existed at all was a disturbance in the sand; a gentle flicking here and there, as if something invisible was jumping.

You will try to recreate for the readers the atmosphere of Captain Quantum's Universal Entertainment, its Final Act – the shouts of 'Look!', the spectators leaping from their benches, crowding round the ring. Peering through their scopes at disturbances in the ring's sand. (It did get dusty.) You will write that it was not the tiniest dot, fleck, speck (which might have been imagination) that enthralled: it was the effect Lucille's appearance had on Maximilian.

How did he know she was there? (You have no idea.) Immersed in his own act, his concentration at breaking point to keep his fireflies dancing. But she must have appeared as the count finished: as the dwarves shouted, 'One hundred!', and Maximilian's white silk and sequinned outline disappeared completely into an aggregate, a body of indefinable and limitless reflection of torchlight. (Extraordinary.)

He seemed drawn in his dance towards the spot near the entrance where Lucille The Incredible Shrinking Bearded Lady was standing, drawn to her by some powerful, inescapable force. Perhaps she joined in that dance and moved to the centre of the ring, you will not be sure, but you are sure that you saw him enter a kind of ever-decreasing orbit, circling the ring's perimeter, the air churned by his passing. You will be sure that you saw the spinning plates leave his orbit as he danced, as if he was throwing them one by one to his love. 'Bequeathing her his greatest achievement' you will write, and be proud of your perceptiveness. (Great strides in observation.) He was pulled towards the centre, the spinning discs flying, flying. You will recall peering closely through your scope to see what happened exactly, but the people gathered either side made it impossible to focus clearly. But you will be absolutely sure that the plates escaped his orbit and entered whatever it was surrounding Lucille. If it was, indeed, Lucille. That some prestidigitation (surely?) rendered them suddenly smaller and smaller until they seemed to disappear. You will be sure that he went on and on spinning until all hundred plates, all hundred canes had been swallowed into the centre, and were gone, replaced by nothing but silence.

And you will report the whole honestly and faithfully, with just a little embellishment of the facts. A little like this story, although facts have little to do with stories. You will say that Captain Quantum was to be seen afterwards sitting on the ring's edge, head in his hands. (Poor man.) That Maximilian, the Great, who had finally succeeded in spinning one hundred plates at once, and who had most certainly not left the ring, was nowhere to be seen. And neither were the plates, the canes or Lucille, who seemed to have completed her final shrinking into a negative quantity. Just the dwarves remained with their little rakes, sadly smoothing infinite grains of sand, ready for whatever came next.

Selected Advice for Strangers

1.   Dress code.

1.a   It is mandatory to dress as a beekeeper when visiting the UK for the first time, otherwise how on earth are they meant to know who are the visitors?

1.b   It is the norm for UK citizens to approach anyone on their home territory dressed as a beekeeper and forcibly escort them across the nearest road. It may be that you do not wish to cross that road, but no matter. They will do it anyway, in the spirit of knowing best for the individual what is best for him/her more than they do themselves. It is suggested that you comply 100%. Please remember that UK beekeepers cannot thus wear the authentic kit, or they would be forever crossing unwanted roads. So they resort to dressing as traffic wardens. Thus, you will show your deep understanding of the UK psyche when you, dressed as a beekeeper, approach a beekeeper dressed as a traffic warden, and say, 'Hello … honey?' It never fails.

2.   Societal norms in the UK.

Society on these disjointed islands is built upon the 'Kleiner Chain Effect'. The simplest manifestation is the beekeeper/traffic warden phenomenon. The chain extends, thus: traffic wardens cannot dress as themselves, or they would naturally be confused with beekeepers. Therefore, they dress as vicars. Vicars as doctors. Doctors dress as pantomime dames and so on, until the chain returns, via librarians dressed as undertakers, and undertakers dressed as trapeze artists, back to visitors. (Beekeepers.)

There is no point in learning the chain. The Kleiner Chain Effect is so termed because it is only ever in place for ten days. After that, everyone changes round, so you never know who is who anyway. Except for visitors. (Beekeepers.)

3.   Integration Patterns.

The Kleiner Chain Effect allows for fast integration of visitors into the UK's multi-faceted community.

a)   Intercourse, parts 1 and 2

It is possible that conditions may be right for sexual intimacy. Since the reign of Queen Victoria, regulations governing the stages of sexual intimacy have been in place in the UK. It is advisable to acquaint oneself with these prior to attempting conjugation.

a)   i. Intercourse Part I

In the first instance, select a person from your own grouping. It is notoriously hard to tell whether a beekeeper is male or female, and care should be taken to select wisely to avoid physical damage.

a)   i. subsection 1

Seeking the company of other beekeepers.

It is possible that you will feel isolated at times, behind your veil. This will manifest itself as an ache under the ribs, and a need to be hugged. You may, at these times, attempt to seek the company of other beekeepers.

It is advisable, when seeking company, to wear the veil down at all times. Thus, you may observe without being seen. You will no doubt note that other beekeepers are attempting to observe you. Do not worry. They cannot fathom any more about you than you can about them.

If particularly lonely, you may, on Thursdays only, extend one hand, sans gauntlet, for the similarly ungauntleted hand of a fellow beekeeper.

In parenthesis.

The beekeeper's outfit is designed to protect the wearer against harm from external causes, such as bees. Self-inflicted harm protection is not guaranteed. Once an ungauntleted hand is extended, you must be aware that the touch of another beekeeper can lead to emotional upset.

a)   i. subsection ii. Regulations on kissing. (extract)

Part five. (Beekeepers.)

Subsection A. sub sub section 5Q: (Beekeeper to beekeeper.)

Note the presence of thick veils. Note that you will not be able to see said other beekeeper and, conversely, the other beekeeper cannot see you. You must therefore make the appropriate pre-kissing-beekeeper noises. Noises like 'Hi, hon, gee, I'm lonely…' are perfectly acceptable. Pursing your lips and making squelchy noises are not. (The Brits are sexually repressed. Why do you think they have rules regarding kissing beekeepers in the first place?) Two veils are thicker than one. (Truism.) Each of you, kisser and kissee, will see the world through composite eyes, rather like those of a bee. (Which is very appropriate. The British love empathising with small fluffy things. Bees are small fluffy things.) The attempt at kissing may well end in tears. Be prepared. But not to worry … thanks to the veil, you never know when a beekeeper is crying.

Generally, the effects of seeing the world through a veil have not been analysed. It is thought, however, that there will be no lasting damage done through your perception of everything cut into tiny squares. The brain is adept, we believe, in reforming the total picture almost perfectly. Almost.

a)   i. Intercourse, Part 2

Let us suppose Part 1 is successful. A touch of ungauntleted hands and a kiss have not led to tears. It has been attempted successfully at least twenty times. (In Huddersfield, reduce that to ten.)

The beekeepers are now ready to attempt further bodily contact. It is strongly advised that the complete uniform must be worn at all times during this manoeuvre. It will be noted that certain bodyzones become heated prior to and during this exchange. Please note that beekeeper outfits can be purchased in modern thermo-reactive material for the uninitiated.

The sensitive, fully clad beekeeper will realise that the above manoeuvre could be described as disappointing. The manual agreed at the time of Queen Victoria terminates at this chapter. Updates are available at additional cost.

The beekeeper must now ask him/herself if it is appropriate to let this other beekeeper know that you really want them. Of course, the answer to this is 'probably'.

You can let them know you want them quite simply by saying the following three words:

I – love – you.

There will no doubt be a pause, while a blank-veiled face waits to reply. Or not.

Do not assume anything. It is kinder on the heart.

Extract F: Airport procedures for beekeepers.

Check in at least two hours before departure. Get searched by a security guard, dressed as a steeplejack. Or by a steeplejack dressed as a ballerina.

Join three other rejected beekeepers. Sit, holding your head in your hands, waiting for your flight to be called.

Wonder where home is.

End of selected advice.

Literary Analysis

Line 1 of text to be analysed:

Earnest and Ruth are sitting on a bench at the station.

Before we go on, stations are points of departure, yes? Or a point on a journey. Earnest and Ruth are not contemporary names ... ah! They are perhaps mid-way through life? This is a point on their journey? An important point, for it to be starting a story. Oh, this is so exciting!

I've just seen – they are together. It is Earnest AND Ruth. There will be a relationship between these two, mark my words.

And – they are SITTING! This is meaningful. They do not stand, they sit. Are they old, to be sitting? Maybe their knees hurt? That is important information, for no writer plants suggestions unwittingly. This should not be discounted. Their knees hurt. Bad knees!

A bench, not a seat. Benches have no back – you cannot fully relax on a bench, can you? So, there is no leaning into each other, this couple – no leaning back, forgetting. Or, perhaps, the author intends us to think they are magistrates? So clever! Let's file that one away for future reference in case the story gets carried away, goes too fast and gets fined for speeding.

THE station. THE. Symbolic, important that THE station has no name, then? OK – a generic station. I knew, just knew this had meaning. It is a generic station, a stopping, a starting, or mid-point on life's journey.

Back to their names – ah – the author has chosen Earnest for him, Ruth for her (supposing that they are indeed the supposed gender, one can't tell – but stick with supposition for the moment). One man, and one woman? Oh, what trails the mind wanders down with 'Earnest'. Is he a deeply serious man, for example? Is he related to Hemingway? Is he good in bed?

Hang on – I'd better explain where that came from. Look – the last four letters spell 'Nest'. Nest is synonymous with 'Bed', therefore the author was thinking of sex and sex is communicating itself subliminally to the reader via Ear 'Nest'. He is serious about bed. Or seriously good in bed. But has a bad knee (see above) therefore he sits.

But what of the 'Ear' of Earnest? We are meant to think of ears of corn, perhaps? Is he a country man? Or maybe he is deaf? We already know he has bad knees ... yes, bad ears. No – only one ear is mentioned in Earnest. So, to recap – this character is good, serious about bed, deaf, but only in one ear, and has a bad knee. Such communication!

Wait. What about *The Importance of Being Earnest*? Another layer for the astute reader. So – not only is he good, serious about bed, deaf, but only in one ear, and has a bad knee, but he is also an important person, perhaps? And wait – what about 'Being' in this context? Is our Earnest just acting, then? Is this man, Earnest, sitting here at this station not really who he seems to be? Does yet another path open up? He is pretending, acting out a role – he is a spy? NO – an actor!

To recap: Earnest is half-deaf, serious about bed, OK at

sex and an important actor, with a bad knee.

Wow!

What about Ruth? His companion, perhaps. Ruth – a Biblical allusion, no doubt? She is, perhaps, religious? A nun? Does she act too – acting out this fantasy for Earnest, in bed?

The meaning of 'Ruth' is 'Pity'. Are we meant to feel pity for this Ruth? Or does she perhaps pity us, having to read this story which starts with her and Earnest on a bench at a generic station? Should we pity her being with Earnest? Should we pity her earnestly? Is she sitting on his deaf side, perhaps?

That's it! He's not listening to Ruth because he can't – not with that ear. Poor, poor Ruth. And stations are such noisy places, too.

Ruth – the gleaner. The picker-up of dropped ears of corn (more ears – ah such cleverness – the weaving is amazing). And yes! Earnest was a man from the country, remember? The author is thus using symbolism to underline the country-ness of both people, here, on this bench and this station.

So, what do we have. Ruth and Earnest, up from the country, she on his deaf side, but – she chose to sit that side, did she not? Her natural place, where she talks and he doesn't hear her. AH!! This is a story about non-communication. I can tell.

Back to the opening sentence, then? To recap: Earnest and Ruth are sitting on a bench at the station.

Continuation of Line 1 of text:

Earnest is eating a ham sandwich.

Oh, God. Ruth MUST be Jewish. Or not hungry. Or he's only bought one sandwich, or…

Feel free to extrapolate at will. So long as you do it in private.

Snakes and Ladders – Creative Writhing

It is a little known fact, Cedric, but fact it is nevertheless, that when snakes are born, they are straight. Like little twigs, or twiglets, pencil-cased together, often born in bundles of six.

You will not remember this, of course, being an older twiglet – sorry, snakelet – for another little known fact is that a snake's memory only begins at three weeks, two days, enough time to get the creative writhing out of the way. Yes, writhing classes for snakes. Without that, my dear Cedric, the life of a snake would be different.

Let us consider. You are eighteen feet long, and have never had the benefit of writhing lessons. You are permanently stuck in a straight line, a long straight line. How do you climb trees? How do you slither along the ground? It costs, Cedric – people make money out of snakes who cannot writhe. Articulated joints are not cheap, and the market is cornered by unscrupulous hyenas. Writhe-free snakes can climb stairs easier than trees, they can manage right-angled bends every foot or so, depending on tread width, rise height.

Your late Uncle Cuthbert, God rest his soul, was such a snake. Banished into the wilderness because he went missing over the period of compulsory interconnected writhing and spent the rest of his days progressing to various positions on a Snakes and Ladders board. Died celibate, Cedric, unloved and unlovable.

Why? Boy, if we snakes cannot writhe, only articulate, (blasphemy, but needs must when you teach) we cannot interconnect. How can an articulated snake make love? Whoever heard of articulated copulation? Thus, Cedric, the act which ensures successful procreation, the passing on of our snakely heritage, is impossible. Uncle Cuthbert watched others from afar writhing most creatively, and he wept. I tell you this in hushed tones. A snake on a Snakes and Ladders board must never weep, Cedric. It gives us away. It is the only way for snakes, doomed to permanent articulation, to survive for more than a year, otherwise we would be food for blackbirds, then magpies, buzzards, eagles and then the great Frigate Bird, who flies in from the western skies. I shiver, Cedric. Fetch me a hot rodent.

Your Uncle Cuthbert fell in love, Cedric. He had progressed to the sixth level. His head was in a blue square numbered sixty three, and his tail curled nicely round number nine. He caught sight of Cynthia. Yes – your mother. Her shining sides, the way she twitched her tail, the little sideways movement of her head when she tasted the air with her perfect tongue. Cynthia was known for her writhing in her younger days. You wouldn't credit it now, would you – but then she was the sexiest snake in the neighbourhood. He saw her, and he slipped. His head dropped into fifty seven, his tail poked right off the side of the board. And he was nearly caught. Managed to hoik himself back, but he cried – and that's how they knew he was a real snake, and that's why they called the Fire

Brigade – and poor Uncle Cuthbert was lost, lost in a deluge of foam, and never seen again.

One of the skeletons in the cupboard, Cedric. It is good that you know. It is good that you have learned to writhe creatively. Find yourself a partner who can writhe as well as you (you take after your mother, Cedric, you really do). You can never writhe too frequently in my opinion.

Writhe, Cedric, writhe. Practice makes perfect, or so they say.

Revisiting Luther

For nine weeks and two days, Letitia Hooper started each morning upside-down, talking to her first husband through the bars of his cage. Wearing a very elderly and baggy black leotard, she would unhook the cage from its stand and place it on the rug, and then she would do a headstand against the wall of her bedsit over the Tatler Tearooms.

'Luther,' she'd say between clenched teeth. 'This is not getting any easier.'

And it wasn't. At sixty, the sinews protested a bit, but so what?

Luther would rattle his beak against the bars or sometimes, if he was in a particularly good mood, put his head on one side and reach over to ting his bell. Parrot or no parrot, suffusing the head with blood for ten minutes every morning was very good for the brain. There may have been some changes to her routine now that Luther was here, but yoga was not negotiable. He'd come to stay under completely false pretences. Never again would she give in to a plea from another librarian to look after a parrot for three months. If she'd known then what she knew now...

As soon as she saw him (he was called Bill then), she knew there was something funny. Not that she was all that well acquainted with parrots, but it was something in his look that reminded her of the first Luther. Bulging eyes and swivelling head, probably. No, the revelation, such as it was, had come later that same day. It was when she'd been undressing for bed. As soon as she peeled off her pants, the parrot set up a frantic whistle and fixed its beady eyes on her pubic hair. Not a wolf whistle, more of the noise a train makes when it rushes into a tunnel at speed.

It was discomforting, being fancied by a parrot. Sitting in bed with her book that first evening, trying hard to concentrate on *Sons and Lovers* for the third time, Letitia had watched him bobbing furiously on his perch, climbing the bars with his knobbly feet. Are parrots sexual beings viz-à-viz humans? Sex with Luther, the Man, hadn't been inspiring; D.H. Lawrence would have been most alarmed. Following the same train of thought, 'Letitia and the Parrot' did not have the same ring as 'Leda and the Swan'. Do parrots even have penises? Letitia got out of bed and went to have a look. She bent down in her winceyette nightie behind Luther, so that her face was at the level of the parrot's rear end, but she couldn't see anything. Then she inspected his lower front. There were too many feathers. The parrot turned round on his perch, and bent to look her in the eye. Letitia blushed. From then on, she dressed and undressed in the bathroom.

Letitia had put her face up close to the bars and eye-balled the parrot, who gazed back at her, unmoved.

'I don't think you're Bill,' she said. 'I think you're Luther Carstairs come back to haunt me.'

The parrot had put its head on one side, and lifted a large seed to its mouth with a claw. No direct answers.

So evasive. Just like Luther the Man. It rolled its eye, and moved the black pebble that was its tongue slowly round the seed, then cracked it, letting the husk fall to the bottom of its cage. It lent forward and looked at the mess it was making. Housework. He was telling her to clear up after him. No question about it. So the parrot became Luther.

Ursula-Who-Does-The-Breakfasts came up with her tray the next morning, 'Morning, Mrs Hooper. Tea and toast. Oh goodness. What's that?'

'I think he'd better have a kipper,' said Letitia in a strangled voice from a few inches above the rug. Luther the Man had had kippers every day for six years. That would nail it.

After yoga every morning, Letitia would usually sit reading the paper over breakfast. This was normally, pre-Luther the Parrot, a quiet time, time to stretch her long legs out from the little settee, and lean back with a cup of tea, while scanning the daily disasters. (Why on earth couldn't the papers print good news for a change? You can't even go on holiday these days without wondering if you'll be blown to smithereens on the way. And forget about relaxing in your own home. The contents of the average food cupboard have been discovered to be a veritable health hazard. Don't think you can escape damnation with going organic either. Last night's organic broccoli had included a large, well-fed caterpillar that had plopped, cooked and rigid, onto her plate.)

Breakfast with Luther was interesting. Parrots have a habit of eating kippers very messily indeed. Letitia had to give up the middle sheets of her newspaper to protect the rug from flying fish, he was loving the kippers that much. She had to be careful though. The kippers had a loosening effect on Luther. He had taken to lifting his tail and shooting a stream of excreta out at whatever happened to be behind him. The first time this happened, he hit the decanter, totally deliberately, of course. Luther the

Man had been teetotal since he went Bahá'í the year before they split up, and Luther the Parrot seemed equally starchy about alcohol. When Letitia poured herself a small schooner of medium sherry after walking up the hill from the library on the Monday evening, Luther went berserk. Even if parrots can't do mock faints and fall backwards deliberately off their perches, Luther came pretty close. He dropped to the ground, and dragged himself round the floor of his cage limping, watching Letitia over his shoulder.

It is all very well having your first husband back with you, thirty years later, even if he is wearing feathers. But it is worrying. There was nowhere to put him where he was not overlooking the bed, other than the bathroom, and going to the loo would have been impossible with Luther watching. So Letitia left him where the librarian had put him, in the corner of her bedsit, by the window.

The other permanent guests of the Tatler Tearooms were accommodating as far as Luther went. Letitia played it correctly, right from the start, and asked them all in to meet him. Of course, she did not divulge to little Colonel Etherington that this was her husband, but she might as well have done.

'Good God. What a sight,' was all the Colonel said. On reflection, Letitia agreed. And the Misses Cartwright. Luther could screech as much as he liked. They were so deaf he didn't bother them on that score, but he did disgrace himself by spitting sunflower seeds into their tea when Letitia seated them too close to his cage.

Mrs Carmichael, the owner of The Tatler, was ambivalent. 'So long as the customers aren't disturbed,' was all she said.

The weeks went by, and Letitia received two postcards from the other librarian, on sabbatical in Florence. What freedom, what stimulation, unlike Letitia's own recent experience. Luther the Man had become impossible to live with all those years ago, and Luther the Parrot was following suit. Their relationship was becoming dangerously similar in many respects to what it had been when he was a man.

After taking off his covers, she gave him his kippers, and the room smelt of them all day. He said very little during breakfast, but then neither did she. She ate her toast, and Luther rasped occasionally and flicked fish about onto the newspaper. She cleared up after him. When she was dressed, he said very little. Often he didn't even bother to look at her, but preened himself instead. Letitia went to work in the library and when she got home, he didn't so much as ask how her day had gone. If she was late giving him his supper he would sulk and turn his back on her. If her hand reached out for the decanter, he squawked like a banshee. It took a while before Letitia realized what the large brown blanket the other librarian had brought was for. And until she did, Luther the Parrot whistled at her all night, bobbing furiously, giving her very little pleasure indeed. Exactly like Luther the Man.

Parrots must know when they are disliked. One day, arriving back from the library, Letitia found three rather nice feathers on the rug. Not little accidental feathers, large ones. Over the course of a few days, a small bare patch appeared on Luther's chest, and more feathers appeared on the rug. That was all she needed. A parrot with psychological problems. The patch grew as their relationship declined.

The countdown to eventual freedom having begun, with only three weeks left to Luther's repatriation, Letitia was devastated to receive a phone call from the other librarian, begging for another month's board and lodging for his pet. Luther screeched throughout the call, making it impossible to hear properly.

'So you'll be back when?' said Letitia over the din.

The other librarian said something about him sounding

as happy as a pig in something or other.

'Yes, but the noise, the intrusion, seriously, when will you be back…?' but he had rung off, and was no doubt off to enjoy a glass of something cool, light and bubbly. Letitia turned to Luther. She would put the blanket over his cage early tonight, and finish her book in peace. She was reading a very good book this time, short stories by Graham Greene. Much more satisfying, short stories, when you have a parrot. Less chance to lose the plot. And anyway, they were like an excellent glass of sherry if drunk at the right time. Left you with a bit of a glow. Luther the Man had been trying to be a writer. Waste of time, really. You were surrounded by books all day at the library, with boxes of the things arriving every Monday. Did the world really need more, especially Luther's? Had he made it after the divorce? She'd never seen anything by Luther Carstairs, but then he might have used a nom de plume.

Seven more bloody weeks. Noise, mess, and the constant reminder of a failed sex life, while she had been young enough and energetic enough to be really good at it, given half a chance. Plus the added cost of all those kippers.

Then Luther made a mistake, a very silly mistake. He turned his back on Letitia, and raised his rump, and before she could do anything about it, he'd defecated all over Graham Greene.

A parrot's neck is much thinner than it looks, through all those feathers. It took Letitia precisely half a minute to wring it. Bloody bird. Ten a penny in the pet shop. There seemed to be feathers all over the room, and Mrs Carmichael wanted to know why she needed to borrow the Hoover at seven on a Thursday evening, but Letitia said she'd spilt some parrot feed. Graham Greene was quite unreadable.

The brown blanket stayed over the cage the next morning. Ursula-Who-Does-The-Breakfasts didn't notice a thing, as Letitia welcomed her, upside down as usual, and said: 'Just leave his kipper on the floor. He's still asleep.'

The day before the other librarian returned, Letitia rang the fifteenth pet shop in Yellow Pages, and discovered that to her delight and relief, they did indeed have a parrot that closely resembled Luther. What she had not bargained for was the cost.

Walking back up the hill from the bus station to the Tatler Tearooms, the new parrot got heavier and heavier. Her bank account had gone in the opposite direction, and was much, much lighter. Several thousand pounds lighter. But the new parrot looked exactly like Luther, and so chances were that the other librarian would never notice the difference.

The new parrot was in its new cage. Letitia settled down on the settee with a new book, *Best American Short Stories*, and a cup of tea. No, damn the tea, a drink was called for. She put down the open book, got up and went over to the decanter.

And the new parrot began to screech. And it screeched, and it screeched and...

Naming Finbar

This is a story about Finbar Dermot O'Flaherty.

Not Finbar Donald O'Flaherty, mind, whose brother Colm, the one with the port wine stain on his left cheek, ran away with a fisherman's wife from Bantry and had to emigrate to Texas … Finbar Donald O'Flaherty who was good at woodwork at school, married a girl from Holland he met in Texas, and went into the clog making business, remember? Not that one.

Finbar Dermot O'Flaherty was born under a gunnera plant by a wet roadside in Kerry on a late Thursday afternoon, only the second child, up until that moment, of the sweet but rather too willing daughter of a mostly drunken travelling family by the name of O'Connor.

Not, you understand, the mostly drunken O'Connors of Castletownbere, who were the prime cause of the burning down of the bookshop. No, not those O'Connors. Those O'Connors don't live in caravans, so how would you think it might be them? No, this is the O'Connors who live in caravans … not the Vincent O'Connors, mind, who have well groomed horses … this is the O'Connors with the smaller caravans and the donkeys.

And that was the main cause of the misfortune that surrounded the birth of Finbar Dermot O'Flaherty, for his mother, the sweet and rather too willing Nathalie O'Connor, after she had wrapped Finbar up in a red and lilac knitted shawl, and after she had taken several swigs from the nearest bottle to dull the pain, announced that Finbar Dermot was not to be an O'Connor, as she thought the name was unlucky.

'I christen this child,' she said, wiping her legs with leaves, and taking another swallow of the whiskey (for that is what it was, a bottle of good single malt purloined by accident from a passing shop), 'I christen this child Finbar Dermot O'Flaherty.'

Tom Seamus O'Connor, her father, not the Tom Seamus O'Connor from Dingle, who built a turf house on the island and lives as a hermit only coming back to the mainland every five years ... and not the Tom Seamus O'Connor who fell into a bog on his way home from his own wedding to Phalaenopsis Flynn, and was never seen again (but they are hoping his body will be recovered in centuries to come, complete with the brand new wedding ring he borrowed from his best friend, Michael) ... Tom Seamus O'Connor, her father, the biggest, roundest Tom Seamus O'Connor this side of Cork, the strongest most drunken Tom Seamus O'Connor to have been in jail for a month and no-one knows why exactly ... was not amused.

'Call the child Finbar Dermot O'Flaherty? The devil you will,' he said, and he retired into the lead caravan to investigate the second bottle of single malt to have been purloined by accident from the passing shop.

The family, knowing full well how Tom Seamus O'Connor could be in circumstances such as these, fled, leaving young Nathalie with her red and lilac bundle to reflect on this momentous thing, all on her own. Nathalie reflected in the only way she knew. She took another swallow of the whiskey, and sat on the caravan steps, watching dusk fall.

Now had she been less rambling and less sweet, Nathalie might have muttered, 'Niggardly old father,' under her breath. Or indeed, 'Decrepit case for euthanasia if there ever was one.' Instead, she whispered loudly, 'Father, you are an old fool.'

Alas and alack. Tom Seamus O'Connor was not as hard of hearing as she had hoped. Unlike the really deaf Tom Seamus O'Connor from Killarney, who did not hear the new mechanical peat cutter coming until it was too late, and the slightly less deaf, but still deaf enough Tom Seamus O'Connor who was banned from Mass by Father Patrick for singing 'Happy Birthday' because he was confused by all those candles … no, her father Tom Seamus O'Connor heard her every word.

'Right, that's that,' he said, coming out of the gloom of the caravan, and descending like a veritable holocaust on the steps where poor Nathalie was sitting. 'You know what's coming now, young lady.'

'Ah shit,' said Nathalie.

'It's the gusset factory for you, my lass. O'Mahoney's Gussets in Tralee. We'll drop you off on our way through, and pick you up in December.'

'But father,' said Nathalie, her eyes filling with tears, clutching her bundle to her chest… 'Father, please, not the gusset factory … terrible, terrible things happen to girls at the gusset factory, Father. Why, remember Sinead Flannery? Oh Father, only two weeks and she ran away to become a nun. Please, not the gusset factory, give me one last chance?'

'OK,' said Tom Seamus O'Connor, sitting down on the step next to his daughter, and taking his latest grandchild on his knee.

''Tis a fine evening to be sure,' he said, rocking the sleeping Finbar Dermot O'Flaherty, and raising his eyes to where the very first star had appeared in a flawless Irish sky. Nathalie sensed a moment of epiphany was approaching.

For a moment, she was quiet. Then, 'Father?'

'Aye?'

'Father, why may I not call the child Finbar Dermot O'Flaherty? For to be sure, it is a fine name.'

Tom Seamus O'Connor sighed and began adjusting the shawl round young Finbar. 'To be sure,' he agreed, 'it is a very fine name and, to be sure, names are important. They define who we are, and what people remember us for. However...' the shawl fell apart and the baby kicked its chubby legs in the breeze, 'this, Nathalie, is a baby girl.'

'Ah,' said Nathalie. 'So Finbar's not a good name, then?'

Tom Seamus O'Connor thought for a moment. Then he shrugged. 'Ach, to be sure,' he grinned. 'Whoever heard of a wee girl called Finbar? Maybe she'll have more luck than we did.' He raised his bottle.

'A toast,' he said, holding the wee girl over his shoulder. A wee girl they called Finbar Dermot O'Flaherty.

Chapter XXXVIII – Conclusion (and a little bit of added cookery)

with abject apologies to Charlotte Brontë

Reader, I did not marry him.

Oh, it would have been an interesting enough wedding, quiet of course, no guests save the bride, the groom, the parson, the clerk. And I dare say, when we got back from church, I might have gone into the kitchen, where Mary would have been cooking the dinner, John cleaning the knives, and I might have said–

'Mary, there's a thing. I seem to have married Mr Rochester this morning!' But I did not. Mary, therefore, had no cause to look up and stare at me: and the ladle with which she was basting a pair of roasting chickens had no cause to hang suspended in air for a minute or so. Nor did John's knives take a similar rest from the polishing process.

I did, however, enter the kitchen, unwed, on my way to fetch a vase for the daffodils. I did listen unwillingly to a basting Mary who mumbled:

'I seed you go out with the master; I thought you was gone to church to be wed…' And John, when I turned to him, was grinning from ear to ear.

'Nah,' he said, sucking his tooth. 'I telled Mary how it would be. I knew you wouldna do it, Miss!' and he politely pulled his forelock. Why do men do that? It is most mystifying.

I did not react instantly, however, just smiled that slight smile for which I am known, and said, 'Thank you, John. I am gratified indeed.' I searched about in my tippety-pocket. 'Mr Rochester told me to give you and Mary this…' I put into his hand a notice of impending redundancy. Dear Mr Rochester had finally enrolled at a cookery school, and would have no further need of Mary's concoctions.

Without waiting to hear more, I left the kitchen. In passing the door of that sanctum some time after, I saw Mary and John still poring over the paperwork, and I caught the words – 'You worked un oat, yet, Mary? Bugger me and I wish I'd larned to read and noat juss mouth in this unfathomable accent what do not transfer willingly-like to t'page.'

I wrote to Moor House and to Cambridge immediately, for I was witholding something vital, reader, for the conclusion. Diana misread my letter, however, construing that I was now a married woman. She announced that she would just give me time to get over the honeymoon, and then she would come and see me.

'Get over the honeymoon?' said I to Mr Rochester, 'Why, what does she think we might have got up to had we wed? Which we have not, but had we – oh I am only a simple girl!' then I pondered this last, adding, 'But an intelligent one, that must not be forgotten…' and another addition, 'rather perspicacious…' and yet another 'and above all, modest…'

I read her letter to Mr Rochester, as his latest cookery magazines, which he had been so looking forward to, had not arrived – it being so far out here, for the poor postman.

'I cannot think,' he cried, similarly nonplussed. 'Blanche

Ingram always said I had a lot to learn.' He shook his head, and waved a recipe for stuffed quail at the wall. 'I thought she meant I could improve my French.'

Dear Mr Rochester. At some point we will have to read up on all this, but, for now, I was glad to lend an ear to his bewailings.

'Oh, Jane…' he seemed lost in reverie. Then he looked up, his face a mask of incomprehension. 'And Bertha too, such a fiery temperament. I am told my lack of skill in the rumpy pumpy department contributed to her indisposition … she went quite mad in the end.'

'Telling me,' I said. 'The curtains on the spare room bed have never recovered. Nor has Thornfield Hall, come to that.'

He hung his head. 'Oh I tried. But they never came out of the oven right…'

'What didn't, light of mine eyes?' I enquired.

'Rumpies,' he said. 'My very own interpretation of the rum baba recipe handed down by my great grandmother. Rochester Rumpies.'

I sighed. 'Something tells me we certainly do have a lot to learn.'

He returned to our latest missive from Diana. 'She does not mention her brother. How is he? Does he write to you?'

I told him – how St John received any news I don't know, as he never said when he wrote, just sent a copy of his latest sermon. Indeed, St John has maintained a regular, though not frequent, correspondence ever since: he hopes I am happy, and trusts I am not of those who only mind earthly things. I advised him to drop the affected 'St' from his name, and be content to be simply 'John'. I wrote thusly: 'It is quite possible that your good Lord would not approve of those who canonise themselves before their demise.' He did write back immediately, arguing his case most eloquently, and it was not until I pointed out that a man called simply 'John' was fairly important in the Bible did he relax and concur.

You have not quite forgotten little Adele, have you, reader? I do try, for she is such a pain, but I cannot; I soon asked and obtained leave of Mr Rochester, to go and see her at the school where he had placed her. Her frantic joy at beholding me again moved me to leave her there for a further year or two, for she had not changed. She looked pale and thin: she said she was not happy, she talked non-stop, mostly about herself. However, I relented. I found the rules of the establishment were too strict, its course of study too severe for a child of her age, and anyway, a girl-person, what would such learning do but place her outside the norm? One ought not be beautiful, rich and well-educated. Education belongs to the plain of face, like moi. See, je can speak le Français.

I took her home with me. I meant to become her governess once more, but I soon found this impracticable; my time and cares were now required by another – my plans were bearing fruit. So I sought out a school conducted on a more indulgent system, and near enough to permit my visiting her once a term, and bringing her home sometimes, in the holidays. I took care she should never want for anything that could contribute to her comfort: Mr Rochester made a habit of baking a different cake each week, and it was despatched to Adele by phaeton. She soon settled in her new abode, became very happy there, and made fair progress in her studies, but sadly, if unsurprisingly, she still had no friends.

As she grew up, a sound English education corrected in a great measure her French defects; where once she had been non-pc, over-excitable, bolshy, and lacking any sort of moral compass, when she left school, I found in her a pleasing and obliging companion: docile, good-tempered and well-principled. By her grateful attention to me and mine, she has long since well repaid any little kindness I ever had in my power to offer her.

My tale draws to its close, reader: one word respecting my experience of married life, and one brief glance at the fortunes of those whose names have most frequently recurred in this narrative, and I have done, and will repair to the withdrawing room to partake of a small glass of raspberry cordial with my beloved.

Mr Rochester continued cooking until his concoctions were the talk of society. Oh, yes, he was completely blind for the first two years, and occasionally, mistook ingredients, with the most amusing results. His sardine and raspberry soufflés, sent to Blanche Ingram's for her wedding, caused mayhem, but then she always needed a rocket up her bustle, don't you think?

It was one afternoon in the downstairs pantry, when I realised his blindness was lifting. Until that moment, I had been his vision, and had naught changed, I would still be stuck at his right hand. Literally, I was (what he often called me) the apple of his eye. But oh, it was such a pother. He saw books through me; and oh: how I did weary of gazing for his behalf, and of putting into words the effect of field, tree, town, river, cloud, sunbeam – of the landscape before us; of the weather round us – and impressing by sound on his ear what light could no longer stamp on his eye. The only fun to be had was in invention – I would turn on the faucets in the laundry room, have him stand by an open window, and declare us to be transported to the very top of the highest waterfall in the district. 'You durst not, move, my dear Mr R,' I would declare. 'Stay still. I will return by nightfall…' and I would withdraw for the rest of the day to indulge in more pleasant pastimes.

Oh how did I weary of reading to him; how did I weary of conducting him where he wished to go: of doing for him what he wished to be done. Was this the only reason why I was on this earth? He claimed these services without painful shame or damping humiliation. He loved me so truly that he knew no reluctance in profiting by my attendance: he felt I loved him so fondly that to yield that attendance was to indulge my sweetest wishes. But oh, dear reader, how wrong, how very wrong he was.

One morning, at the end of the two years, as I was writing a letter to his dictation, filling it with deliberate spelling mistakes, he came and bent over me, and said – 'Jane, have you a glittering ornament round your neck?'

I had a gold watch-chain, but, petulantly, I answered, 'No.'

'And have you a pale blue dress on?'

I had, but said it was yellow. He informed me then, that for some time he had fancied the obscurity clouding one eye was becoming less dense; and that now he was sure of it. He and I went up to London. He had the advice of an eminent oculist; and he eventually recovered the sight of that one eye. He cannot now see very distinctly, but enough to no longer make marmalade and basil soup or serve roast pomeranian for dessert with crème anglaise … he cannot read or write much; but he can find his way through a simple recipe for dropped scones without being led by the hand.

My Mr R and I, then, are happy of a sort: and the more so, because those we most love are happy likewise. Mary Rivers married: once every year, she and her husband, Mr Wharton, come to see us, and we go to see them. Mr Wharton is a clergyman, a college friend of her brother's, and, from his attainments and principles, worthy of the connection, although he cheats at rummy and bathes only once a quarter. We plan our visits carefully.

As to St John Rivers, he left England: he went to India. St John is unmarried: he never will marry now. (Who would marry him, reader? Look at the verbiage up with which one would have to put.) Himself says he has hitherto sufficed to the toil, and the toil draws near its close: his glorious sun hastens to its setting. I am told this means his life nears its end, although why on earth we do not use simple language and resort instead to euphemism beats me.

We are all most relieved to be settled, finally. The last letter I received from St John drew from my eyes human tears (as opposed to crocodile, perhaps?) and yet filled my heart with divine joy: he anticipated his sure reward, his incorruptible crown. Typical. Each to his own, I say. Crowns have never sat well on me – one's hair, caught back in a simple but tasteful bun, would never suit.

And now, mine own conclusion. Dear reader, I was promised a visit from Diana Rivers, you will recall. And she came, pretending joy at my supposed marrriage to Mr R. Her proximity and my bounding heart would not allow the maintenance of deceit – in no time at all, our love for each other was declared, and we now live together in companionable and consummate bliss. We have to put up with Mr Rochester in a ménage à trois, and his obsession with truffle-hunting for his esparragos con trufas is hard to bear. But that is a small price to pay for true happiness.

A Short History of Synchronised Breathing

or

How the Tail of the Crocodile Became the Head

(Dear reader – please feel free to choose the better title. Whichever title you choose, this story comes with deepest genuflections to Aesop, the legendary father of storytelling.)

Once, many years ago, so many years that the mathematicians have not yet invented a number large enough, there lived a man with an extraordinary capacity for breathing. I kid you not. He lived on the very edge of a vast city at the foot of the tallest mountain in the world – but that is well nigh irrelevant – the information is only here to lend some concept of incomprehension.

(I am very sorry this story begins with a secondary character. The main character is also secondary, at least at the beginning.)

Every morning, he would stand on his balcony, take in the deepest, most masterful lungful of air through his nose, feeling it percolate to every extremity, each molecule fizzing with potential, which it delivered with the most satisfying efficiency. Then, its task completed, the spent air would exit his body as smoothly as it had entered. Through his mouth. But that was not all! The first lungful finished, he would repeat the process over and over again, each intake as well-balanced as the last, each exhalation the very pinnacle of equilibrium.

> (He was also married. His wife was a perfectly nice woman who does not feature in the story any further than this sentence. It could be said that her whole life was lived in parentheses.)

In the house across the way, there lived another man whose life was not quite so measured. He had fifteen children with twenty-three wives – or perhaps it was twenty-three children with fifteen wives – the exact details are lost, but he was most certainly fertile, and very busy. As a result, on many mornings, he would go outside and lean against the wall of the house with a glass of sweet tea, escaping the commotion caused by thirty-eight souls (or thereabouts), swill the tea round his teeth, and after he swallowed, he would cough. Only the very smallest of coughs. Nothing sinister, and certainly not enough of a cough to bother the neighbours, but a cough all the same.

> (Another secondary character, I'm afraid. I really am breaking all sorts of rules here. However – rules are made to be broken, as someone once said. You have a few more paragraphs to wait before the important person appears. But this one is a catalyst and has therefore earned his place...)

Opposite, the man with an extraordinary capacity for breathing

> (Let's call him Norman for simplicity from now on.)

had the most acute hearing, caused by the extraordinary efficiency with which molecules fizzed to his every extremity, including his ears.

'Friend,' he said, in a conciliatory tone (for, being perfectly polite, he did not wish overly to intrude, but what man, given a natural advantage, would not wish to impart a little of that advantage to others?). 'Friend, I divine that your respiratory system is wanting.'

His neighbour paused in his swilling of sweet tea round his teeth, glanced sideways at Norman, whose ribcage was expanding with air yet again, and spat on the ground. 'Look, watch and take note,' said Norman, inhaling through his nose, so that the air fizzed even more and hissed against the little hairs in his left nostril with a sound like water escaping from a crack in a cistern.

As luck would have it, a crocodile was passing.

(Sorry for the wait. The main character has now arrived! Bear with me, please.)

I said, a crocodile was passing. Not, of course, a denizen from the banks of the Nile or any other fluvial source – but a crocodile of young children walking two by two, led by their teacher.

'Open your mouth,' exhorted Norman, intending his message for the ears of his neighbour. But the children, used to responding immediately to an order, opened their mouths. The whole crocodile, boys at the front, girls at the back. Including a small girl, who had no-one to walk with, and always brought up the rear, hence her nickname, The Crocodile's Tail.

(Really sorry for the wait. This small girl is the heroine of the story.)

'Inhale like this,' ordered Norman from his balcony, breathing in with such force that his lips puckered most alarmingly and his chin juddered on its hinges. His chest expanded, and expanded, until he resembled a swaggering pigeon. The children breathed in as one, until they resembled two parallel rows of pigeons with a small, but potentially very important, Tail at the back, headed by a larger pigeon, for, of course, their teacher was also following orders.

'Feel the air waking up your very extremities,' ordered Norman. (He must have breathed out to give the order, but that fact is not recorded specifically.) 'And hold!' He held his breath. The whole crocodile held its breath as well, including The Crocodile's Tail, until one girl towards the back fell over in a swoon. '…and out!' ordered Norman, exhaling down his nose. The crocodile followed suit, and the resulting hiss could be heard half way up the mountain.

(This was indeed recorded by a passing monk. On parchment. I ought to make it clear our heroine did not swoon. She was tougher than that, even at such a tender age.)

'Do you not feel marvellous?' cried Norman. 'Is your body not fizzing with energy? Your mind with new ideas?'

'It is, they are, we am!' chorused the crocodile (apart from The Crocodile's Tail, who was far too young to tackle the tenses). And for the next hour or so, they breathed most efficaciously in formation, conducted by their teacher. What about the fertile and busy neighbour? Not recorded.

And that was the start of it. The children breathed in and out very deliberately all day, taking notice of the fact. They returned home that evening and spread the method to their nearest and dearest, who picked up the new skills very quickly – and little else was talked about for three days.

(I hasten to add that our heroine did not do this. The whole class had been breathing along with her rhythms, anyway. At home, she found that the family were all breathing perfectly OK without her interference, thank you very much.)

Of course, there were those for whom the new breathing was not easy. Break a task into its component parts and it becomes a thing precisely of its component parts and nothing more – each part necessitating concentration, acknowledgement, external affirmation. But soon, after multiple delegations from the furthest quarters of the city, and the offering and acceptance of a few gold coins, Norman agreed to hold regular teaching sessions to ensure delivery of standard instruction in his breathing method, city-wide. And everyone was so delighted, they pronounced that he should be the de facto Prime Minister.

Imagine the sights. Whole neighbourhoods inhaling and exhaling at once, so much so, indeed, that in the wooded areas, the resulting air currents were sufficient to waft the branches of the trees to and fro. And the flags on the gathering places, the skirts of the women, the hair of the wives of the three chief speakers in the halls of justice – all whipped about as if in a constant hurricane. Imagine the sounds. The whole city breathing at once, filled with the rush of several thousand airways. Imagine.

(Our heroine took to reading, to ward off constant attacks of the giggles, as this all reinforced to her, young as she was, how very silly was the world of grown-ups.)

It was not long before Norman was offered a dwelling with a balcony overlooking a great open space, right at the heart of the city. And every day, at three separate appointed hours, he could be seen breathing on his balcony, the expanse beneath filled with citizens watching carefully and hanging on his every breath. Three hours a day became four, five six, as demand for tuition increased, and as the word spread, visitors came from far and wide to learn how to breathe in this most exemplary and extraordinarily capacious fashion.

(Years are passing. Our heroine is growing up, and she just happens to breathe as required by the new – or not so new, by now – custom.)

Six, seven, eight hours a day. Enough. Norman was soon so much in demand that he was in danger of spending every waking hour in passing on his gift to others. He must delegate! Recruit helpers. Those for whom breathing had become almost as second nature as Norman's own breathing was to him. Notices went up across the city, meetings were held, the exact experience and qualifications needed to teach breathing were discussed, and discussed again. The notes from these preliminary discussions were torn up, the subject debated again, and again – until after many months, if not more, the exact and precise criteria having been identified, a proper campaign could be carried out, and the most suitable candidates recruited to carry on the good work.

Nineteen men were, in the end, appointed to be tutors of breathing.

(There were twenty, but one got so excited at the prospect that his breathing rhythms broke ranks with the rest at a most vital part of the recruitment procedure, speeded up alarmingly, and he hyperventilated before being disqualified.)

So – nineteen tutors, headed by Norman, now living in the most sumptuous surroundings, and appointed Professor of Inhalation at the city's most prestigious university, as well as the de facto Prime Minister. And the tutors, naturally, appointed themselves his Deputies, de facto.

(Years are still passing. Our heroine, still living peacefully, is now studying at the same university, learning the rich culture and turbulent history of her city and, indeed, her nation, and its various dialects and all neighbouring languages, breathing quietly to herself through her public examinations, which she is passing with flying colours – generally improving herself at every turn.)

(This is now a sad bit. Please get your handkerchiefs

ready…)

In time, Norman reached the end of his appointed days, and his legendary breathing, extraordinary capacity or not, ceased. It happened like this – he had chaired a single debate. (Single because he was the only qualified debater.) He had given three lectures on the only topic possible. He had followed the lectures, as was his habit, with a demonstration for the benefit of first year students, standing on a plinth on the lawn in front of the main building.

'In, hold, out. In, hold, out.' The rhythms were underlined by the chronicler of the day, whose job it was to verbally keep pace with the ins and outs. 'In, hold, out. In, hold … hold … hold … hold … Professor?' For of course, everyone listening was also holding their breath and their faces were turning various shades of red, then blue. Professor Norman then toppled sideways and fell off his plinth, (so the records state) to land, in mid-inhale, on the grass, where he expired, his ribcage at full expand.

(Of course, the whole city was devastated, with the exception of our heroine, who had too much studying to do, and always thought the city's obsession with synchronised breathing totally impractical.)

Norman's funeral was an occasion to surpass all occasions. His pallbearers, chosen in three teams of four from among the nineteen tutors, carried his coffin on their shoulders in a most grave progress through the city. It must be said, the coffin was the oddest shape, having been constructed especially to contain a man who, in life, was not considered small of girth, and who, in death, thanks to rigor mortis setting his ribcage for eternity, necessitated the deepest funerary receptacle ever made in those parts. Imagine the scene, the pallbearers with that weight on their shoulders, the chronicler of the day going on before, intoning, 'In, hold, out … in, hold, out…', to assist them in their task.

Imagine too, the twentieth would-be tutor (he who was

rejected) hiding in an alley, seething with jealousy, but breathing with enhanced control thanks to the intervening years spent doing nothing else but practising it twenty-four hours a day … planning, and plotting between the absolute perfection of his ins and outs.

(Our heroine caught a glimpse of both the procession and the seethings of the would-be tutor, from an upstairs window overlooking the same alley. This story is indeed fraught with coincidence. Her only thoughts were, 'How silly…' then she returned to her manuscripts.)

The funeral rites went on for days, the neighbours mourned and 99.999% of the citizens mourned, but only after the priests give their solemn permission for the occasional break in the rhythms of breathing, to allow for the odd hiccough, the odd sob, the odd wiping of the nose with a linen handkerchief. The university mourned, and while it mourned, began to formulate plans for the selection of the next Professor of Inhalation (who would also be the de facto Prime Minister).

How to approach such a momentous decision? As before, meetings were held, the exact criteria for the appointment were discussed, and discussed again. The notes from these preliminary discussions were torn up, the subject debated again, and again, until finally, the simplest solution was discovered, proposed by a student who happened to be passing the debating chamber on her way to the library.

(This is of course, our heroine.)

'You need a person with an extraordinary capacity for breathing. Why not choose from among the tutors, whoever's capacity is the most extraordinary?'

The room fell silent. And the discussion quickly turned to the extreme logic of the proposal, and its inherent impossibilities. How to measure such a thing as air, when air is invisible? The debate became louder and louder, sweet tea was brought, and hot compresses. And it was not until the same student, passing by the debating chamber on her way back from the library, shook her head and said just two words, 'Pig bladders…' that the matter was resolved.

(Straight to the point, and somewhat tongue-in-cheek, but…)

It was not a good time to be a pig. Nineteen identical bladders were extracted (records do not go into details about their procurement…) from nineteen identical pigs. And the ceremony approached at which all nineteen pretenders to the throne of Professor of Inhalation (and de facto Prime Minister) would vie for the position. The great debating chamber was packed when the day arrived, and the hour. All nineteen processed around the room, then lined up, lips pursed, bladders at the ready. But before they could blow in synchronicity, the doors were flung open, and in marched the twentieth would-be lecturer – he of the previous hyperventilation – holding aloft, yes, his own pig's bladder, procured from a twentieth identical pig. 'My qualifications are such,' he announced, between deep, even breaths, 'that I claim the right to compete for the position…'

Of course, there was no basis for quibbling, so no quibbling was heard. And at the count of three, with a single deep inhalation, all twenty men blew into their bladders. (well, not their own, obviously) and slowly, the bladders inflated to their identical maximum.

('Well, that's a lot of use,' muttered the crowd, but, of course, that's not part of the story…)

Apart from one. Nineteen inflated roundly and shiningly – but the twentieth, oh my goodness, that bladder at first seemed to stop at the same pressure as the rest, but then imperceptibly, as the twentieth man continued to exhale rhythmically and strongly, his bladder continued to expand, until it was fully twice the size of the rest. And indeed, he continued to exhale, stretching it even further, until suddenly, the bladder burst with an almighty bang.

There was uproar. There were shouts of 'Professor!' and 'Prime Minister!' There was no need for further ceremony, and the twentieth man was proclaimed the winner.

But.

(There is always a 'but' after elections, don't you find? This one was no exception.)

No sooner had he been enthroned than he stood on the Professor's plinth, and declared that he be not only Professor and the de facto Prime Minister, but Emperor. And King. And Managing Director. And Chief. And Official Winner of Everything. And indeed all other roles that came to mind. Including Colonel-in-Chief of the Army.

Now this country had lived through centuries of peace, and the army was a rather pleasing lot who spent most of their time marching and breathing in formation, putting on displays of the same in a parade ground that was also a vast and beautiful display of seasonal planting, in co-ordinating colours. And, of course, they were initially delighted to be headed by such an eminent fellow – who immediately, and without delay, drew up Rule Books governing all organisations and all sectors of the populace – including an Army Rule Book, the ignoring of which was punishable by asphyxiation. No-one quibbled. All the rules were based on synchronised breathing, and that seemed reasonable enough.

(Reasonable enough to most people, but, to our heroine, this began to smack of something unhealthy. She kept an eye … and although she has been a secondary character for most of the story, things might be going to change soon.)

Populations that breathe as one, armies that do not fight but march among flowerbeds. You are no doubt wondering how long this could last, and you would be quite right. For not long afterwards, the city was invaded by barbarians who had the temerity to breathe differently. As need arose. Oft-times, through nose and mouth together! The army, under strict orders not to break ranks under penalty of asphyxiation, did their best to fight off the intruders, but sadly, outdone and exhausted, they failed on several fronts. There was a pause in the battle, and the city's soldiers, exhausted, were seen to gasp and to break their accustomed rhythms.

Unfortunately, the new Professor, Prime Minister, King, Emperor, Official Winner of Everything was passing, ready to inspect his troops. He noted this lack of discipline. This dreadful insubordination. 'General asphyxiation for all miscreants, this afternoon…', he ordered, and that was that. No thought for the invaders, or anything else.

Of course, the only place big enough to asphyxiate the major portion of an army was the university, the lovely open spaces, so preparations were made, and hundreds of coffins were found from somewhere and brought to the university in readiness.

Our heroine, of course, enquired what was going on.

(The time is fast approaching when she will take on a more visible role … like you, dear reader, she has seen the fundamental flaws in the plan, and might soon come out from her parenthetical position.)

'Excuse me,' she said, 'but if you asphyxiate our army, then who will fight for us?'

The Prime Minster (etc., etc.) snorted. 'Logic has no place here, my dear. This is about synchronicity, and control…'

'Really?' she said. 'And you do this breathing yourself?'

'I do,' he said. 'What else is there?'

The Crocodile's Tail shook her head. 'I don't believe you.'

'Then you shall be asphyxiated too,' he announced, striding to the podium, strangling ropes at the ready.

By this time, everyone had fallen quiet, and even

though our heroine spoke in a small voice, it was heard. 'I can prove it…'

There was a gasp.

(Synchronised, of course.)

Her words fell on fertile ground. 'What? Our great leader? He does not breathe with synchronicity?' The terrible possibility spread through the throng. And spread.

'Of course I do,' retorted the great man, pulling the strangling ropes tight between his fists, and gesticulating at our heroine. 'Asphyxiation time! You first.'

She did not even flinch, but said, 'You do not breathe with synchronicity when you are asleep … Sir.'

His protests were in vain. The city set up a vigil (a pause in the invasion having been negotiated), and waited for the great man to go to sleep. They followed him for four days, while his eyelids grew heavier and heavier, and he continued to breathe strongly, just as they did, in rhythm. But on the fifth day, tiredness got the better of him and he fell asleep. Not even in bed, but on the pavement.

(How are the mighty fallen! How they crowded round to listen, and how his breathing became shallower and shallower, as he fell into the broken rhythms of sleep. And as dreams overtook him, his breathing responded to his unconscious. Speeding up when he was aroused, as I'm afraid he was, fairly frequently. Slowing when he was calm. He even snored, and had a touch of apnoea, but that isn't strictly relevant…)

'She is absolutely right!' they chorused. And I hardly need tell you what happened next. Yes, the army broke ranks, went off to fight the barbarians and routed them completely, thanks to their newly rediscovered ability to organise necessary air supplies without even thinking about it. The whole city, and further, tentatively at first, started to breathe individually. And when no-one died of it, the word spread – 'We're free!'

(Actually, they had been free before, but people are
funny – they do like to be led. Sometimes…)

But there was a new panic. The Prime Minster (etc., etc.,
etc.) had disappeared – and who blames him? There is
nothing so foolish as a fool at the top – but who would
now be leader? Who would govern? And no-one wanted
the responsibility at all. No-one. Until, of course, our heroine said she would do it, if that was OK. And if everyone
didn't mind, and were in agreement? For she had a few
ideas, and had studied a little.

(For years, reader, years!)

There arose a chorus from among those who were quietly
enjoying the freedom of non-regimented breathing – 'That
would be fine, but…'

(Here, I gather she declined to allow the speakers to
finish. But it is also recorded that she did not seek to
embarrass them. Instead…)

Our heroine explained she would select her advisors and
colleagues based not so much on how they breathed, this
time, but rather based on revolutionary ideas such as how
much they understood the city, and the nation, and its
position vis-à-vis others. 'Love of not only its past, and
present, but its future,' she said. 'Its culture. Its history. Its
economics … and many more surprising things like that.'

But sometimes, people are difficult to please. The chorus continued:

'How will you govern? What will be the central tenet?
The era of Synchronised Breathing has ended. What now?'

There were fearful glances all about, for, as everyone
knows, a vacuum cannot remain such, and will fill itself if
nothing comes along to do the filling.

'I have plenty of ideas,' said our heroine,

(who we must now name – over to you, dear reader.
Name her…)

'Tomorrow, we shall have a meeting, and we will discuss and debate the options. We will decide together which is best for us, for our children, and our children's children.'

'Yes but,' chorused the Deputies, reverting in their anxiety to quasi-synchronicity of inhalation. 'We shall not rest unless we have a little more information to help us sleep. Our heads have been so full of the challenges of breathing that we fear there will be room for little else for a while. Give us a clue?'

'Of course,' said the new Prime Minister,

(or insert here the name you have chosen...)

'We will govern entirely by metaphor.'

And that was such a wondrous pronouncement that afterwards the Deputies all slept very well indeed, in the fulsome knowledge that they were about to become part of something perfectly logical, if utterly and completely incomprehensible.

Skellig

Where the old stones do not quite meet, high on the outer terrace, Michael is watching a gannet, brilliant white in the distance, following the grey horizon east – west. The air is filled with sounds of sea birds, the bird sounds are filled with the ceaseless noise of the ocean, the ocean noise with the sound of his heart beating. How can he hear his heart over the pounding of the waves on the rocks below? For a moment, the whole island tips. Skellig Michael, the island that carries his name.

Michael joined the party late, as they were boarding the ferry. No-one checked his ticket, or took a name. He stayed apart on deck, tucking his hands into his sleeves to keep his fingers warm. No-one bothered him, or called him to join them in the cabin for the pre-landing talk – 'Sea Birds of the Skelligs'. The last of the thirteen licensed day trips allowed this year. He stayed on deck, his jacket the colour of the water, the colour of distance.

Michael steadies the island by pushing his foot against a stone. A large stone, the guidebook says, is the foundation of an edifice, perhaps the shelter of hermits. If he leans out, looks down, he can see where the nests are. Storm petrels, the souls of sailors lost at sea.

Most of the party wanted to photograph the puffins. Up vertiginous steps cut eleven centuries ago, their surfaces polished by time and the footfall of countless monks. Pausing by the dry stone clocháns, where a woman had hung behind, her voice rising after them as she sang some old plainchant, the sound belling up, being snatched and blown about by the wind, until Michael wasn't sure it was the woman's voice at all.

There are plenty of fallen stones. There are places where the rainwater has collected in hollows. There will be more rain, daily, now, maybe constant. Michael pulls his collar up. There is grass. Sparse, but some. Moss in the north-facing channels. There might have been some wild garlic on the first terrace. There are limpets on the rocks, mussels, other shells. There are the puffins. Kittiwakes. Guillemots on the other side. There are places where a man can climb down to the nests, if he is careful.

The bird watching party went down past the monastery walls, stepping with care where the ground was uneven. They set up their tripods, their telescopes, jostling for the best positions, conversing in angry whispers. The guide shouting over the tension, 'Back at the landing stage in forty five minutes.'

Michael turns round, and leans against the old wall. Below him, down the steepest steps, is the second terrace, with its tumble of unmortared stones someone said was once an altar. The guidebook says it was a burial place, the stones a cairn. Up here, to be buried up here, in the air, almost in the sky. A half-hearted stone placed on a chest, a token shrouding, food for the sea eagles.

Somewhere, there are the remains of an oratory. You could rebuild an oratory higher, here, looking west. Where you could close your eyes against the last rays of the sun and hold its light fixed against your retina until dawn.

Later, from his vantage point high in the hermitage, he watches the party picking its way back across the ruins, down and down the steps. He sees how small they become. How their colours fade into the evening. How their voices disappear, and become part of the sound of birds, the wind and the sea.

The island tips. Michael jams his foot against the stones, turns and looks down at the ledges far below where the storm petrels nest. The foretellers of storms to come. There are none there now, they will be flying far far out in the Atlantic, part of their ceaseless journeying. He bends and picks up a stone, weighing it in his hand. Petrels. Peter's birds. The walkers on water. He places the stone on the old broken wall, and starts to rebuild.

Acknowledgements

My gratitude to the following publishers, editors and organisations for commissioning, and/or publishing, and/or broadcasting, and/or causing to be performed, some of the stories that are collected herein:

Tales of the Decongested, Foyles, Charing Cross Road ('How Claude Romarin Lost the Buttocks of Celestine Bigorneaux'), British Council/European Union National Institutes of Culture, Athens ('A Short History of Synchronised Breathing', first published in Greek translation), Lakeview International Journal of Literature & Arts ('Parallax'), Salt Publishing's Overheard anthology ed. Jonathan Taylor ('Ed's Theory of the Soul'), Unthank Books' *The Red Room Anthology, stories inspired by the Brontes,* ed. A.J. Ashworth ('Chapter XXXVIII: Conclusion'), BBC Southern Counties/ Guildford Book Festival Short Story Competition ('Naming Finbar'), Defenestration ('Revisiting Luther'), One Page Stories ('Pavel's Grey Painting'), The Café Irreal ('Were It Possible to Just have Sustenance'), BBC Radio 4 ('Housekeeping'), Freight Books' *I Am Because You Are* anthology, ed. Tania Hershman and Pippa Goldschmidt, celebrating the centenary of Einstein's Theory of General Relativity ('Captain Quantum's Universal Entertainment'), World Literature Today (Skellig), The Seventh Quark ('Literary Analysis'), Smokelong Quarterly ('Wei-Ch'i').

Enormous thanks to Paul McVeigh for laughing in all the right places and saying very generous things about this book, and to Maria McCarthy and Bob Carling of Cultured Llama.

Cultured Llama Publishing
Poems | Stories | Curious Things

Cultured Llama was born in a converted stable. This creature of humble birth drank greedily from the creative source of the poets, writers, artists and musicians that visited, and soon the llama fulfilled the destiny of its given name.

Cultured Llama aspires to quality from the first creative thought through to the finished product.

www.culturedllama.co.uk

Also published by Cultured Llama

Poetry

strange fruits by Maria C. McCarthy
Paperback; 72pp; 203×127mm; 978-0-9568921-0-2; July 2011

A Radiance by Bethany W. Pope
Paperback; 70pp; 203×127mm; 978-0-9568921-3-3; June 2012

The Strangest Thankyou by Richard Thomas
Paperback; 98pp; 203×127mm; 978-0-9568921-5-7; November 2012

The Night My Sister Went to Hollywood by Hilda Sheehan
Paperback; 82pp; 203×127mm; 978-0-9568921-8-8; March 2013

Notes from a Bright Field by Rose Cook
Paperback; 104pp; 203×127mm; 978-0-9568921-9-5; July 2013

Sounds of the Real World by Gordon Meade
Paperback; 104pp; 203×127mm; 978-0-9926485-0-3; August 2013

The Fire in Me Now by Michael Curtis
Paperback; 90pp; 203×127mm; 978-0-9926485-4-1; August 2014

Short of Breath by Vivien Jones
Paperback; 102pp; 203×127mm; 978-0-9926485-5-8; October 2014

Cold Light of Morning by Julian Colton
Paperback; 90pp; 203×127mm; 978-0-9926485-7-2; March 2015

Automatic Writing by John Brewster
Paperback; 96pp; 203×127mm; 978-0-9926485-8-9; July 2015

Zygote Poems by Richard Thomas
Paperback; 66pp; 178×127mm; 978-0-9932119-5-9; July 2015

Les Animots: A Human Bestiary by Gordon Meade, images by Douglas Robertson
Hardback; 166pp; 203×127mm; 978-0-9926485-9-6; December 2015

Memorandum: Poems for the Fallen by Vanessa Gebbie
Paperback; 90pp; 203×127mm; 978-0-9932119-4-2; February 2016

The Light Box by Rosie Jackson
Paperback; 108pp; 203×127mm; 978-0-9932119-7-3; March 2016

There Are No Foreign Lands by Mark Holihan
Paperback; 96pp; 203×127mm; 978-0-9932119-8-0; June 2016

Short stories

Canterbury Tales on a Cockcrow Morning by Maggie Harris
Paperback; 138pp; 203×127mm; 978-0-9568921-6-4; September 2012

As Long as it Takes by Maria C. McCarthy
Paperback; 168pp; 203×127mm; 978-0-9926485-1-0; February 2014

In Margate by Lunchtime by Maggie Harris
Paperback; 204pp; 203×127mm; 978-0-9926485-3-4; February 2015

The Lost of Syros by Emma Timpany
Paperback; 128pp; 203×127mm; 978-0-9932119-2-8; July 2015

Only the Visible Can Vanish by Anna Maconochie
Paperback; 158pp; 203×127mm; 978-0-9932119-9-7; September 2016

Who Killed Emil Kreisler? by Nigel Jarrett
Paperback; 208pp; 203×127mm; 978-0-9568921-1-9; November 2016

Curious things

Digging Up Paradise: Potatoes, People and Poetry in the Garden of England by Sarah Salway
Paperback; 164pp; 203×203mm; 978-0-9926485-6-5; June 2014

Punk Rock People Management: A No-Nonsense Guide to Hiring, Inspiring and Firing Staff by Peter Cook
Paperback; 40pp; 210×148mm; 978-0-9932119-0-4; February 2015

Do it Yourself: A History of Music in Medway by Stephen H. Morris
Paperback; 504pp; 229×152mm; 978-0-9926485-2-7; April 2015

The Music of Business: Business Excellence Fused with Music by Peter Cook – NEW EDITION
Paperback; 318pp; 210×148mm; 978-0-9932119-1-1; May 2015

The Hungry Writer by Lynne Rees
Paperback; 246pp; 244×170mm; 978-0-9932119-3-5; September 2015

The Ecology of Everyday Things by Mark Everard
Hardback; 126pp; 216×140mm; 978-0-9932119-6-6; November 2015

Lightning Source UK Ltd.
Milton Keynes UK
UKOW03f0309040417
298287UK00002B/10/P